MURDER BETWEEN NEIGHBORS

Murder Between Neighbors

A Write Club Mystery

by

Michelle Corbier

Books by Michelle Corbier

Write Club Mystery series

Murder Is Revealing

Murder In Gemini

Mwindaji series

Dark Blood Awakens

Standalone novels

Hollow Voices

Michelle Corbier
415 Pisgah Church Road PMB 342
Greensboro, NC 27455

For more information: www.MichelleCorbier.com

This is a work of fiction. Names, characters, places, brands, media, and incidents are either the product of the author's imagination or are used fictitiously.

Book cover design by ebooklaunch.com.
Murder Between Neighbors

ISBN: 979-8-9903308-0-1 Murder Between Neighbors, eBook
ISBN: 979-8-9903308-1-8 Murder Between Neighbors, paperback
ISBN: 979-8-9903308-2-5 Murder Between Neighbors, audiobook

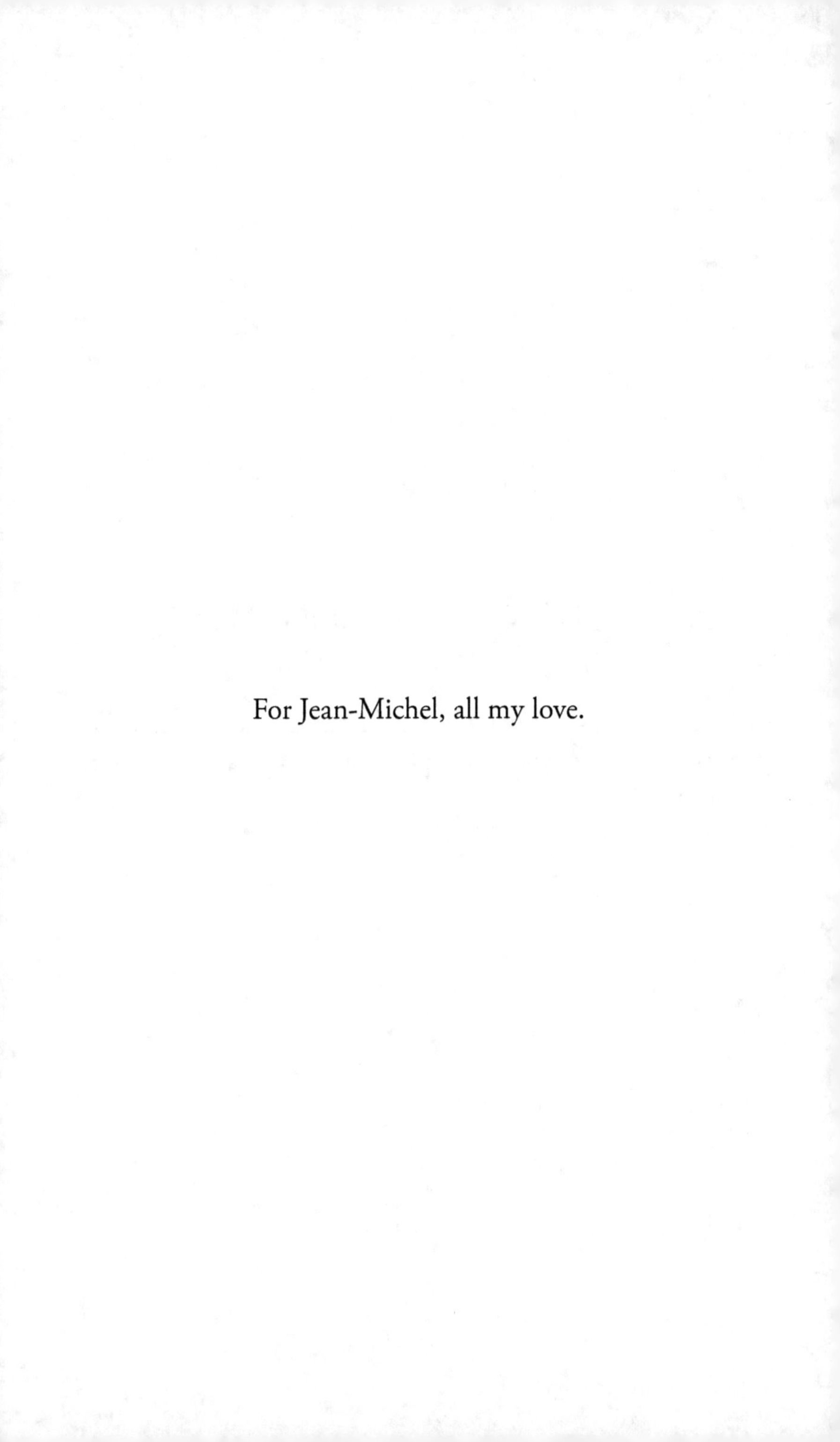

For Jean-Michel, all my love.

Acknowledgements

Special thanks to my family and friends who encouraged me every step of the way—particularly Maria for helping with the Spanish verses.

PROLOGUE

The doorbell rang, interrupting Jared's workout. Inside the garage which doubled as a gym, he hit the mute button on the television remote, grabbed a water bottle from the mini refrigerator, and headed for the front door. With a high-pitched squeal, the doorbell rang two more times as he entered the house.

"Who is it?" he yelled, glancing through the peephole. Before opening the door, he chugged from the water bottle.

"What the hell are you doing here?" he asked, entering the kitchen and tossing the empty bottle into the trash can.

Silently, the front door closed as his guest followed him.

In the kitchen, Jared swiped a beer bottle from the refrigerator. "Thirsty?" He shrugged when his guest declined. "Suit yourself."

Following his guest into the living room Jared asked, "Where are you going?"

Stoically, his guest sat on the couch facing the front door.

"Make yourself comfortable," he smirked, collapsing onto a recliner adjacent to the couch. He belched. "If you came to beg…"

"I never beg."

He snickered. "If I remember correctly, a couple times you—"

"I'm not here to discuss our past."

"Then why *are* you here?" His polished veneers glistened. "Want some afternoon delight?"

Flinching slightly, his guest said, "I came to give you an opportunity to do the right thing."

After a chortle, Jared finished the beer. "Not likely." He glanced at the bottle before setting it aside. "Well." He stretched his arms over his head and yawned. "Anything else?"

"You should consider the bigger picture."

"There's only one issue." While rubbing his belly, Jared frowned at the beer bottle positioned on a side table next to a lamp.

"You drink too much."

"Go to hell," Jared said, grimacing and massaging his chest.

"You first." His guest rose, ambling around the living room and gradually standing beside a six-foot Christmas tree next to the fireplace.

"I bet you'll feel differently when—" Jared reached for the beer bottle, but only managed to knock it over. He crumpled to the floor, clutching his gut. "Something's wrong with that beer."

"Oh." Swiftly, his guest retrieved the beer bottle from the floor and read the label.

"It's bad." Jared belched and covered his mouth. "I'm gonna be sick." Suddenly, he rushed up and sprinted down a short hallway leading toward the guest bedrooms and into a bathroom. He dropped to his knees and vomited into the toilet.

***

Ten minutes elapsed. Jared remained curled in a fetal position on the bathroom floor. Noise from opening cabinets made him glance up. A minute later his guest appeared in the doorway.

With a dour face, his guest said, "Poor thing. I told you alcohol would kill you."

Sweat dripped down Jared's face and neck. His heart raced, pounding like a jackhammer in his chest. "Call 911. My stomach is about to explode."

Instead, his guest pivoted and left the bathroom.

Dry heaving, Jared summoned his waning strength and army crawled down the hall into the living room. "What are you doing?"

From the floor, Jared watched as his visitor searched the cabinets beside the oversized television on the far wall over the fireplace. "You won't find them," he said, slurring his words.

His guest continued searching, eventually removing a brick at the base of the fireplace. From the concealed cavity, his guest removed a VHS tape. Grinning, they held up the tape. "This?"

"How did you…" Jared used the arm of the recliner to push himself up off the floor but gradually slumped back to the ground. Rolling over, his spine arched, and his limbs convulsed. Spittle and foam dribbled from his mouth.

Giving Jared a mere glance, the visitor stepped over his seizing body and placed the open beer bottle beside his clenched hand.

At the front door, they peeked around the neighborhood. Finding the cul-de-sac empty, they hurried outside and down the street. In the midday sunlight, deflated festive blowup characters littered the surrounding yards with their outdoor holidays lights off.

Christmas might have been two weeks away, but it had come early for at least one person.

CHAPTER 1

Twilight brought a comfortable hush around the cul-de-sac. For a moment, as the streetlights flashed on, everyone appeared suspended in motion. Cold from the descending evening brought an end to the neighborhood festivities. A beat later, activity returned as people began collecting items and returning to the coziness of their warm, snug homes. From a music player, *Please Come Home for Christmas* by Aaron Neville floated along the street.

Myaisha shivered, glancing up at the heat lamp. She touched its metal column. "This isn't working." She zipped up her coat and gathered empty plates from two rectangular tables.

Tiffany, her next-door neighbor also rose. "It's getting late anyway."

Kids playing in the cul-de-sac collected balls and other toys and headed home. Several older children circled the street on their bicycles and skateboards. Observing the children, Myaisha smiled, wondering when her son, Josiah, would return home for college winter break.

He said he'd call. She glanced at her watch.

"So, what about the decorations?" Carter asked, before biting into a slice of pizza.

"You don't have to agree on a theme," Sharon said, sauntering over to the half dozen adults huddled together at the end of Myaisha's driveway. Her home sat at the apex of their cul-de-sac and thus became the de facto hub for all their gatherings.

Sharon stood at the end of one of the larger tables. "The HOA needs to know if your street will be participating in this year's holiday decoration contest. We need a decision today."

"We have this same discussion each year," Jared huffed, drinking from a beer bottle. "And we never reach a decision."

"Sure, we do," Myaisha said, opening a trash bag so he could dispose of the bottle. "Every year we decide not to have a theme and let each homeowner decorate their house as they please."

"We're not displaying any decorations this year," Tiffany said, crushing an empty paper plate and dropping it into the bag Myaisha held. "It's too much effort, and we're busy with work. Isn't that right dear?"

Carter, Tiffany's husband, nodded and glanced over at Jared, who sneered and turned away.

"What about you, Mrs. Lula?" Myaisha asked.

The septuagenarian inhaled deeply and surveyed their cul-de-sac. "I'm not big on celebrating holidays." Mrs. Lula's eyes misted as she gazed distantly.

"We know," Jared said. "You're the only person who doesn't hand out candy on Halloween."

The older woman snapped to attention and glowered at him. "I'd think those hooligans of yours have enough stimulation without adding sugar to their bodies."

Jared began to rise from his chair. "Don't you—"

"Where's your wife, Roger?" Myaisha asked, hoping to lessen the tension.

"Abigail isn't feeling well," he said, clearing his throat. "She has to be careful. The doctor doesn't want her to overexert herself. Wouldn't be good." He rubbed the bottom of his lip with the end of his pipe. "I offered to roll her out here, but she didn't want to catch a chill."

"I understand," Myaisha said. "No one wants to get sick around the holidays."

"Nope. I remember one Christmas…"

As Roger recounted a tedious story about his medical problems, people stirred. Respectfully, Myaisha remained seated, attentively listening to his oft-repeated woe about gout—no, this time he was discussing his bypass surgery. She reclined into the folding chair, prepared to be a good neighbor. *He must get bored, stuck at home all day nursing his wife.*

As Roger's narrative ended, Jared stood, his thin hair blowing in the light breeze. "Let's go, guys," he said, addressing his kids, who were playing soccer in the center of the street.

"Ignore him," Tiffany said, patting Mrs. Lula's wrinkled hand. "We appreciated the Mississippi mud pie you made us for Thanksgiving. You should open a bakery."

"I love cooking," Mrs. Lula said, gazing at Jared's retreating back.

"It's a way to say, 'I love you'," Sharon said, a flush blooming across her pale chest. She quickly averted her gaze as people watched.

"Well, I plan to dish up a lot of holiday treats," Myaisha said, glancing momentarily at her abdominal bulge. "Josiah should be home this weekend." *Why hasn't he called?*

"I'll place my order right now for Mrs. Lula's rum fruit cake," Tiffany said. "Let me know what you need, and I'll supply all the ingredients."

The two women conversed as several adults drifted away. Myaisha watched Jared gather his children and head toward his house.

"Wait a minute." She trotted after him. "Can we discuss the fence?"

Jared grimaced. "What about it?"

She hesitated, measuring his hostile demeanor. "I don't want to be a pest, but my fence still needs to be repaired."

"Then fix it," he snorted. "It's your fence."

"Yes, but *your* kids damaged it."

"The fence is over ten years old—about time you replaced it."

"That's not your decision," she said, folding her arms across her chest. "Now, I provided you with several estimates. When will you—"

"It's Christmas. Let's discuss this after the new year."

"Exactly, it's Christmastime, and your kids damaged the fence on the fourth of July."

"A harmless prank. Don't be dramatic."

Myaisha's hands clenched. "Since we're neighbors, I'm trying to be reasonable. But if you refuse to help with the expenses—"

"What's the big deal? Why are you in such a hurry?"

"I don't want Boomer to get outside the yard—or another dog to get in."

"If you disciplined your dog—"

"Why don't you discipline your children?"

Jared advanced, glaring into her face. "Don't talk about my kids."

"What's going on?" Patsy asked, rushing outside in house slippers. "Myaisha, is there a problem?"

Gritting her teeth, she pivoted from Jared to face Patsy. "We were discussing the fence."

Patsy's large doe eyes looked at her husband. "I thought you were going to file a claim with our insurance company. Didn't you—"

"Shut up," Jared said, glowering at Patsy, who flushed and cowered.

"I'll get to it when I have time," Jared said, stomping away. "And if that's not good enough," he sneered, his gaze boring into Myaisha's, "then sue us."

He slammed the front door shut.

"Sorry," Patsy said, before scampering inside the house behind her husband and children.

Myaisha stared at the house, mumbling several of the more creative curse words she'd learned from her ex-military dad. A minute later, she turned toward her house. *In the morning, I will call my lawyer.*

Holding up an empty pizza box, Tiffany asked, "Would you give me a hand?"

"Of course. I got distracted." She grabbed a fresh trash bag and cleared off the tables. "Where did everyone go?"

"Home. Oh, here comes Mrs. Lula with more trash bags." Tiffany whispered, "She's such a sweet woman— too bad she spends the holidays alone."

Before Myaisha could reply, Mrs. Lula came up to them.

"Here, Tiffany. Let me help you with that." Mrs. Lula held open a large trash bag as Myaisha and Tiffany cleared food and other debris from the folding tables.

"For the next block party," Tiffany said, "we're going to have rules about clean up. The three of us always seem to be on cleaning crew."

Stuffing a discarded tissue into a trash bag, Myaisha said, "If you want something done right…"

"Assign a woman," Mrs. Lula completed.

They laughed and continued cleaning.

Thirty minutes later a silence descended around the cul-de-sac. Everyone had departed. House lights came on.

Before she entered her garage, Myaisha peeked over at her next-door neighbor's house. *When did Jared become such an ass?*

CHAPTER 2

Myaisha exited the exam room as an infant began screaming. The noise echoed around the busy medical office, joining the voices of the office staff and patients. She searched the nursing triage room, hall, and staff restroom.

"Where's Dina?"

Yvette, her office manager, shrugged and shook her head. "No idea."

Because her nurse hadn't arrived for work, Myaisha had to room each patient and administer all the vaccinations.

"Of course Dina would be ill on the busiest day of the week."

As Yvette hustled behind her, Myaisha scrambled inside the nursing triage area. While listening to Yvette's complaints about Dina's tardiness, she drew up another batch of vaccinations.

"Today, every patient seems to require immunizations or lab work."

"I called the temp agency," Yvette said. "They don't have anyone available until—"

"Forget it," she said, a tad harsher than intended. "I can handle the vaccines if someone will record vitals and room patients."

Myaisha overheard Yvette giving instructions to the front staff as she entered another patient exam room.

Twenty minutes later when she exited the exam room, Myaisha's shoulders relaxed. Dina had entered through the building's rear door, quickly removing her winter coat.

"Sorry, Mrs. Doctor," Dina said, unwrapping a long woolen scarf from around her neck. "I'll get the next patient ready."

Myaisha rested a hand on Dina's shoulder. "Thank you. It's good to see you."

Dina flinched and Myaisha quickly removed her hand.

"Sorry." She retreated to a private office in the rear of the medical building and collapsed into a plush leather chair. After plugging in her teapot, she charted on the morning patients. A minute later her cellphone vibrated.

"Hello," she said, cradling the phone next to her ear.

"Hi, Mom."

"Josiah." Myaisha stopped typing and relaxed into the leather chair. "I wondered when you'd call. Are you coming home tonight?"

"Umm."

The five seconds of silence felt like minutes.

Her neck tensed and her voice trembled. "What's wrong?"

"Would you mind if I didn't come home for Christmas?"

Thoughts swirled around her mind. *Why wouldn't he want to spend the holiday with her? Did he have a girlfriend? A boyfriend? Were they growing apart?*

"No, I understand." She swallowed hard, barely masking her disappointment. "Is everything all right?"

"Yeah. I wanted to stay on campus and work on next semester's projects."

Myaisha listened as her son—whom she adored—explained why he preferred to stay in Chapel Hill for the holiday, alone, than to spend time with her.

"Well, if anything changes, call."

"Love you, Mom." He hung up.

She stared at the blank cellphone screen. Sorrow swelled in her chest. She barely held back the tears. A Christmas without Josiah. The ache growing in her chest reminded her of their first holiday together after Sammy died.

Christmas dinner had been her husband's favorite part of the entire season. He preferred a big, scrumptious meal to anything she could gift him. Myaisha grabbed a handful of tissues, dabbed her eyes, and blew her nose.

A quarter of an hour later, through her cracked door, she heard giggling. With effort, she ignored the noise and charted. This day had started horribly and now…

Ten minutes elapsed before Dina tapped on the door. "The next patient is ready."

Before she could reply, Dina had departed to care for another patient.

As Myaisha sauntered to the next patient room, laughter from the front office again captured her attention. Puzzled, she approached the reception area.

The craftsman-styled home she'd converted into a medical office had a long hallway dividing the back area. On the right, a rectangular cubicle functioned as a nursing station. Patient exams rooms were positioned on the left side of the hallway.

At the beginning of the hallway, on the left, a half wall looked over onto the reception area. A long low countertop separated the reception area from the lobby waiting area. Seated side-by-side, her front staff giggled and conversed.

"Did you see those gloves she had on?" Alma asked.

"She's crazy," Shirley replied, scratching at her extensions. "You know she spends a fortune on gloves and masks. Dr. Douglas refused to pay for those surgical masks with face shields anymore. Dina even wears gloves when she eats."

Alma laughed. "I'm surprised she hasn't worn off her skin with all that hand washing. She's a freak."

Frowning, Myaisha turned aside and bumped into Dina.

"Sorry. Your next patient is ready," Dina said.

Myaisha hesitated but decided to address her concerns later. Patients first.

A half hour elapsed before she escorted two expectant parents out of an exam room.

"Well, we've heard good things about you," a visibly pregnant woman said. "We're so happy to finally meet you."

Before she could respond, Myaisha heard more laughter. A flushed Dina fled from the reception area into the nursing triage room. Though she caught a mere glimpse of Dina's face, Myaisha noticed her bottom lip quivering.

"Thank you," Myaisha said to the expectant parents. She directed them to check out. "Call anytime. My afterhours number is in the welcome packet."

Once the family departed, Myaisha scanned the lobby. Only one person remained, and she knew he expected a ride. She walked over to the reception desk.

"When Mr. Hopkins leaves, I'd like to speak with you both in my office." Myaisha strode away before the front staff could reply.

Twenty minutes later someone rapped on her door.

"Come in," she said, briefly looking up from her paperwork. "Shut the door and sit down."

The medical assistants retrieved chairs from around the room and sat in front of the long wooden desk. They exchanged a brief glance. When Shirley began to speak, Myaisha raised her hand.

"I heard you two making fun of Dina."

Alma's jaw tensed. Shirley gazed down at her feet.

Scowling at both of them, Myaisha exhaled. "You should know better. Bullying a fellow employee. This is not *Mean Girls*. I won't tolerate this behavior in my office."

Alma threw her shoulders back, and her chin jutted forward. "We were just joking. It didn't mean anything."

Myaisha rested her hands on the desk. "How did Dina react? Did she appreciate your humor?"

Neither medical assistant responded. For a quarter of a minute, Myaisha observed them.

Slouching in the seat, Alma asked, "You want us to apologize?"

"I want to know if this is who you truly are." Myaisha paused and relaxed her shoulders. "If you don't understand the harm your words caused, I misjudged your character."

Alma glanced to the side, pouting.

"I'm sorry, Mrs. Doctor," Shirley said. "It didn't seem… It won't happen again."

Myaisha nodded before turning toward Alma, who avoided her gaze.

"I should hope not." She rose. "Because if it does, neither of you will be laughing in this office again."

She dismissed the medical assistants and returned to paperwork. Not five minutes had elapsed before Yvette knocked and entered, closing the door gently behind her.

"Is everything okay?" she asked, dropping into one of the chairs in front of Myaisha's desk.

"Maybe." She tossed a pen aside. "Is Dina in the triage room?"

Wide-eyed, Yvette leaned forward eagerly. "Yeah, but I let the front staff go out for lunch."

"That's fine." She glanced at the wall calendar. "We need to have a staff meeting—before the holiday break. "Can you arrange it?"

"On it." Yvette rose. "Anything else."

"Before you schedule the meeting, ask Dina to come in."

A minute later, Dina rushed into Myaisha's office. "Yes, Mrs. Doctor."

She smiled, momentarily appreciating the moniker the staff used to distinguish between her and her now deceased husband, who had also been a physician. "Sit down."

As Dina rested in a chair, Myaisha noticed long purple gloves extending past the medical assistant's elbows. For a couple seconds, she considered how best to broach the topic. Prior discussions with the nurse had not ended well. Cognizant of Dina's sensitivities, Myaisha considered a circuitous approach, but fatigue led her to be direct.

"I overheard the staff teasing you."

Lowering her face, Dina said, "It's nothing. They… people laugh because I'm always wearing gloves."

Myaisha circled around the desk and sat in a chair beside Dina's.

"It's not okay—and I told them so."

"But—"

"No one deserves to be teased, humiliated, or taunted." She observed Dina's trembling chin. "I can't stop what happens outside this office, but here you'll be able to work in peace."

A tiny smile creased Dina's dry, cracked lips.

Reaching forward, Myaisha started to pat Dina's shoulder, then withdrew her hand, recalling the nurse's aversion to physical contact. She peeked down at Dina's gloved hands.

"How's your atopic dermatitis?"

Slowly, Dina removed the gloves, displaying her cracked, fissured skin.

Myaisha grimaced, examining Dina's fingers without touching. "Have you gone back to the dermatologist?"

Dina shook her head. "No. The copay is too expensive."

With a sigh, Myaisha circled around the desk. From inside a drawer, she removed her wallet. "How much?"

Gaping, Dina said, "I couldn't. Mrs. Dr.—"

"If you don't use the cream, your hands will bleed. Damaged skin can become infected. Have you considered the injectables?"

For fifteen minutes, they discussed treatment options for atopic dermatitis. Myaisha shared a website where the nurse could review treatment options.

"Have you returned to therapy?" she asked, stashing the wallet in her purse.

"No, I don't want to go anymore. Talking about my past only makes me depressed—and it doesn't seem to be working." Dina turned up her palms, displaying her damaged hands.

Myaisha understood. *Who wants to discuss their history of being abused? But would Dina be able to move forward without addressing past traumas?*

She appreciated the concept of wanting to bury your past. The agony. A temptation to hide it, believing it would miraculously disappear if you didn't mention it. Over the years, Myaisha had attempted many subversive tactics to deny her own heartache. Time brought old wounds to the surface, though. Eventually, the past would refuse to be ignored. She learned that painful lesson after the murder of her college friend, Candace.

"If you want to heal, you have to face what happened," she said. "Look how hard you've worked to overcome your obsessions."

Dina sat up straighter. "I only shower twice a day now."

"See."

"But I can't give up the gloves."

"It'll take time. What about the masks?"

"In the office—not outside anymore," Dina answered.

"That's real progress. I'm proud of you." She approached Dina. "But you have to continue with therapy."

Together, they exited her office.

In the hallway, Myaisha asked, "Are you going to lunch?"

"No, I thought I'd make up my time by working through the break."

She nodded. "Of course."

Myaisha started to reenter her office but pivoted around. "And, Dina, if you need anything—money, support—let me know."

"Thank you, Mrs. Doctor," Dina said before skipping down the hall.

For a moment, she watched Dina moving about. She needed to be more observant. *How had she not seen this ugliness creeping into their office? The cruelty between her medical assistants and nurse.*

She had always appreciated a good relationship with her staff. *When did things change—and why hadn't she noticed?*

Myaisha massaged her neck and returned to her office. A calendar reminder pinged on the computer: *'Call lawyer.'*

Between her catty office staff and Josiah not coming home for Christmas…

"Damn Jared. He's going to fix my fence, or else."

CHAPTER 3

Because she neglected to slow down, Myaisha took the turn into the cul-de-sac at twenty-five miles per hour. Tires screeched and she reflexively slammed on the brakes.

Straight ahead, her house loomed. A police patrol car was parked in front of her mailbox, next to an animal rescue unit and a half dozen neighbors. Since the patrol car was blocking her driveway, Myaisha parked next door on the right, in front of Tiffany's house. She jumped out of the car as the engine stopped.

"What happened?" she asked, rushing over the crowd of spectators.

No one answered. She noticed a couple neighbors, off to the side and huddled together, mumbling amongst themselves.

She spotted two uniformed police officers. One had a gun pointed at Boomer. A man wearing a white jumpsuit, with the words ANIMAL CONTROL printed in orange on his jacket, held a long metal pole with a looped leash on the end.

Circling around the crowd, Myaisha dashed over to the growling, bristling black Labrador. "Boomer!" She threw her arms around his neck.

"Stand back, lady," the police officer ordered, aiming his gun at Boomer. A second animal control officer sat in the rescue van, talking over a radio.

"This is insane," she said, panting from her brief sprint.

Slightly lowering his gun, the police officer approached. "We received a call about a rabid dog."

"Boomer isn't rabid." Her gaze bore down upon the neighbors. "Who called?"

"Doesn't matter," the officer said, addressing her but his gaze fixed on the Lab.

One of the animal control officers joined the police officer speaking to Myaisha. "Is this your dog, lady?"

Standing beside Boomer, Myaisha directed him to sit. "Yes, he is—and he is fully vaccinated and licensed."

While this discussion took place, the second police officer exited the patrol car. She watched him walk over to Jared's house. Following her gaze, Boomer remained at attention but zeroed in on one person. Jared stood at the foot of his driveway.

"Did *he* call?" Myaisha asked, pointing her chin toward Jared.

"Ma'am," the police officer drawled, "I told you, it doesn't matter. Your dog got loose and bit—"

"Bit who?" she gaped, bringing Boomer closer to her side. Her eyes strained, scrutinizing Jared's body for blood or torn clothing.

Wearing sweats and sneakers, Jared lunged forward. "Me. That beast should be put down."

She rushed toward Jared. Boomer hugged her side. One of the police officers stepped between them, causing her to stop a few feet away.

Myaisha's heartbeat hammered in her ears along with a tiny warning voice repeating the same refrain, 'You're going to jail.'

Slow down. Think. If you get arrested, Boomer gets locked up too—maybe worse.

"If Boomer bit you, it's because you did something to him."

"I was home, minding my own business when he attacked me," Jared said, his neck veins taut against the collar of his hoodie.

"What are you doing home this early anyway?"

"That's none of—"

"Enough!" the police officer shouted, raising his hands and separating them.

An animal control officer approached Myaisha. "We need to see the vaccination records and license for the Lab. If his shots are up to date, you can pick him up at the kennel."

She gasped. "Where? You're not taking him to a pound. He didn't do anything wrong."

"He bit your neighbor," the animal control officer said.

"Boomer didn't bite anyone. Show me."

"We don't have to prove anything to you, ma'am," the police officer said. "If you interfere, I'll arrest you."

Her gaze automatically flew to the officer's weapon. His flat eyes didn't offer compromise. His gloved hand hovered over the gun clinging to his hip.

Swallowing hard, Myaisha said, "Then you'll have to arrest me too. Boomer is on my property, and I don't see any injury to my neighbor."

For a moment, the air was sucked out of the cul-de-sac as if everyone had drawn in a deep breath. Every eye rested on the police officer, who scrutinized Myaisha then Jared.

Despite her strong words, inwardly she trembled. *Should've called Deniece.*

Once she'd received the call from Mrs. Lula, Myaisha had zipped out of the office and straight home. Since she hadn't told Josiah or Deniece what occurred, if she ended up in jail they wouldn't know. *Then what would happen to Boomer?*

He'd be taken to the kennel. And if he acted aggressively, they *might* put him down. Nauseated, she swallowed the bile refluxing in her throat. Straightening her spine, Myaisha rested a hand on Boomer's head, returning the police officer's piercing gaze.

The second police officer questioned Jared. "Sir, where were you bitten?"

Jared stammered. "What? Are you kidding me?" He retreated from the officer. "I'm the victim and you're cross-examining me?"

Assuming a wide stance with his arms draped over his chest, the police officer asked, "Sir, can you prove the dog either bit you, or stepped on your property?"

"What do I need, video proof?"

"It would help," the animal control officer said. "This dog isn't exhibiting behaviors of a rabid animal."

Scanning the crowd, Jared said, "Tiffany."

Like a tornado, Tiffany zipped around and headed toward her house.

"Wait." Jared raised his voice. "Tiffany saw it. Didn't you?"

Faced away from the crowd, Tiffany lowered her head and slowly swung around. She avoided Myaisha's and Jared's gaze, instead looking at the police officer. "I..."

"Ma'am," the police officer said, "if you did see anything, we need to know."

Tiffany's two ponytails danced as her head shook. "I don't want to get involved."

With Boomer at her heel, Myaisha also approached Tiffany. "Please. If you witnessed anything."

The police officer held up his hand and growled, "Step back, ma'am. You're lucky I'm not hauling your behind downtown. One more step and I will."

Myaisha bit back a rejoinder and directed Boomer to sit. She watched Tiffany, her gaze pleading for her neighbor to tell the truth. Jared's clothing appeared intact, without signs of damage. At over one hundred and twenty pounds, Boomer would've torn Jared apart if he had attacked.

"What did you see?" The officer's intense countenance made Tiffany, who continued to avoid Myaisha's gaze, tremble.

Wrapping her arms around her bare arms, Tiffany hesitated. In shorts and a T-shirt, her toned legs flexed, prepared to flee. "Well..."

For a second, Tiffany glanced past the police officer and at Jared. The latter's smug face slightly nodded. Myaisha's shoulders tensed.

They were communicating something anonymously, but what? And why would Tiffany be compelled to follow Jared's lead?

She detected an uncomfortable undercurrent about their interaction. Her body shivered, not from the cold winter afternoon, but fear. *Were they colluding against Boomer?* Though curious, at the moment her concern focused solely on her dog's safety.

Tiffany exhaled, keeping her alert eyes on Jared. "I saw the dog outside in the front yard."

Myaisha squeezed Boomer's collar. Realizing she might be hurting him, she relaxed her grip.

Widening his stance and with one eye on Myaisha, the police officer asked, "Where? In whose yard?"

"From my house it's hard to tell." Tiffany shivered. "It's freezing out here. I'm going back inside."

While the officer followed Tiffany, the animal control officer asked Myaisha, "May I examine your dog?"

Initially hesitant, she consented after directing Boomer to sit. "Be nice. He's a friend."

Boomer glanced up at her with droopy, doubtful eyes before sitting obediently.

First placing his pole inside the van, the animal control officer slowly approached the Lab. It took a minute, but he allowed Boomer to lick his hand before petting the dog's head. Reclining on his side, Boomer let the animal control officer rub his belly.

"This dog isn't aggressive," he said. "Probably scared. How did he get out?"

"My neighbor's kids damaged my fence," Myaisha said, glowering at Jared.

"That's not true," Jared said, scrambling over to the animal control officer.

Once Jared bolted forward, Boomer launched onto his feet, growling and barking.

"See!" Jared screamed. "He's a menace. I'm surprised he hasn't killed anyone yet."

The second police officer addressed Jared. "He doesn't appear to be a danger to anyone but you." He bent down and pet Boomer's head. Eyeing Jared, he asked, "Are you gonna show me where he bit you or not?"

"Screw this," Jared said, storming toward his house. "I'm calling my lawyer, then I'm going to the doctor." Before he entered the house, he shouted over his shoulder. "This isn't over! I'm suing your ass and making sure that monster is put down!"

The police officer who was speaking with Tiffany eventually rejoined his partner. Myaisha couldn't hear their conversation because the animal control officer was speaking to her. When one of the police officers started inspecting the fence, her shoulders tensed.

As the animal control officer departed, one of the police officers approached her.

"Better fix your fence. Mr. Lowry doesn't look like a dog lover." He petted Boomer once more. "I've seen this before. He can make your life a living hell if he wants to. Don't understand people who hate animals, not natural." He departed and sat in the patrol car.

After speaking with the police officer, Myaisha remained in her driveway.

"Ridiculous," Roger gruffed. "Boomer wouldn't bite Jared. He has better taste than that."

Myaisha tried to smile but couldn't. She'd come too close to losing Boomer. Though still afraid, her heart rate had moderated. However, she could feel knots in her neck.

While jotting notes down on a small tablet, the first police officer said, "Mrs. Stilwell isn't sure if the dog got onto Mr. Lowry's property or not. She's coming in tomorrow to give an official statement." He glared into Myaisha's face. "I suggest you fix that fence and apologize to your neighbor." The police officer eyeballed Boomer. "Otherwise, you'll be needing a new dog."

After uttering those last words, the police officer stomped away.

The hairs on the back of Boomer's neck raised.

"Down, Boomer," Myaisha said. "We don't bite police officers, even when they deserve it."

For several minutes, after all the neighbors had returned to their homes, Myaisha stood in her driveway surveilling the cul-de-sac. She glanced right at the house closest to the main street. *Where had Mrs. Lula gone?*

Eventually, she took Boomer inside and collapsed on the couch. She'd thank Mrs. Lula later. Boomer trotted over and laid his head on her lap. Myaisha massaged his neck.

"Don't worry. You're not going anywhere. Mommy would sooner see Jared dead than allow anyone to take her Boomer."

CHAPTER 4

A chilly wind blew Myaisha's thick, curly black hair around her face. She tried—unsuccessfully—to rope it behind her ears. Thick mittens covered her hands, hampering the process. She bounced from leg to leg, stimulating the circulation in her feet.

"Maybe we should do this tomorrow," she said, standing behind AJ.

His words were garbled because of the nails between his lips. "No, I'm good."

"Well, I'm freezing." She shuddered, slid the glove off her left hand, and removed the nails from AJ's mouth. "That's dangerous—not to mention unhygienic."

"Do you want your fence fixed or not?" He took the nails from her and began hammering a long, pale plank vertically along a three-foot gap in the fence. Burn scars covered two wooden slats framing the opening.

She stared at the ground, mumbling. "We wouldn't be out here if Jared simply paid for the repairs. Jerk."

With her shoe, Myaisha prodded the stiff brown grass. She checked her watch. Jared should be home from work. *What would happen if she confronted him with AJ present?*

Firemen helped people. Having a six-foot ten-inch boyfriend should come with advantages. And if Jared got nasty, she could tell AJ to punch him in the face. *AJ's a human being, not a tool.* Besides, she'd rather smack Jared's pointy nose herself.

A pile of brown pellets caught her gaze. "What's that?"

"I don't know," AJ grumbled, positioning another piece of plywood above the first.

Using her shoe, Myaisha rolled the pellets around. On inspection, she discovered more pellets in the grass near the gap in the fence. She picked up a piece and brought it to her nose.

"You're not going to eat it?" AJ winced.

"Of course not. I'm smelling it."

AJ grimaced and hammered in another board.

Snapping the pellet in half, Myaisha sniffed it again. "This is cat food."

"Why would someone sprinkle cat food around your fence?" AJ asked, sending her a quick glance before hammering another plank.

"Maybe to lure a hungry dog out of the backyard." Myaisha stared at the pellet then glared next door at Jared's house.

Thirty minutes later, AJ stood, stretching his back, and handing her the hammer. "There. All fixed."

"Humph." She snorted and headed toward the garage. "Let's get inside. I'm freezing my butt off."

AJ wrapped an arm around her waist. "It looks fine from here."

She ignored his comment as he kissed her neck. In the garage, she hung the hammer on a peg board with other tools and pushed the button to lower the garage door. On her heels, AJ entered the house.

In the kitchen, Boomer and Zoey, AJ's brown Lab, sat beside their food bowls.

Myaisha frowned at the dogs. "We've been outside freezing to make a safe home for you two, and the first thing you do is beg for food."

Zoey woofed and Boomer seconded.

Before she could head for the pantry, AJ poured nibbles into the bowls.

"There you go," he said, patting Zoey's head. "You going to let me pet you, buddy?" AJ's hand hovered in the air above Boomer's head.

The black Lab's low stomach growl preceded AJ's retreating hand.

"No problem," he said. "Maybe one day."

After washing her hands, Myaisha began removing food items from the refrigerator. "Don't let it bother you. Boomer's still upset about yesterday."

The kitchen stool squelched as AJ sat. "Do you actually think your neighbor deliberately lured Boomer outside the fence?"

"Why not?" Myaisha shut the refrigerator with her elbow. "He's an ass. And there's no other explanation for why Boomer would leave the backyard."

"Maybe he was curious."

Myaisha prepared dinner. "Boomer has lived here all his life. What made him suddenly decide to investigate the side yard?" She poured soda into a cup and handed it to AJ. "Besides, I can open the front door and Boomer won't leave the house without my permission."

"Well, he left the backyard for a reason."

"Food." With zeal, Myaisha chopped lettuce. Green leaves flew around the cutting board.

AJ stole a sliced cucumber from the board. "What's with you and this neighbor?" he asked, crunching the vegetable.

Myaisha glared at him. "He called animal services on my dog."

"This wouldn't have happened if you'd fixed the fence. I offered to do it for you. Those planks will at least keep Boomer inside until you hire someone to repair it."

She dropped the knife on the kitchen island, where it clattered. "Are you blaming me?"

AJ's hand rose pleadingly. "All I'm saying is if you fixed the fence, this wouldn't have happened."

"I didn't *break* the fence. My moronic neighbor's kids burned it."

After a deep sigh, AJ circled around the island to stand beside her. "Life is difficult enough without inviting trouble."

Myaisha jerked away from him. "Seriously. You're blaming me for this."

"All I'm saying is, fix the fence and get reimbursement from the neighbor later. Protecting Boomer is what matters."

"It's important to stand up for your principles. His bebe kids broke my fence. He should fix it. I'm not paying for a new fence."

Shaking his head, AJ returned to the stool. "You're not listening. If you'd calm down—"

"What?!"

Both Labs vaulted off the floor at her exclamation.

"I'm simply—"

"I've waited six months to get my fence fixed," Myaisha said as the knife wavered in her hand.

"I offered to fix it several times."

Myaisha gaped. "Outrageous!" She hacked at a bell pepper. "You're saying this is my fault."

AJ's jaw tensed. "You're not—"

"I listened to what you said. Give in and let my neighbor get away with not paying to fix the fence."

"That's not what I said."

"So, what would you have done?"

"Fix the fence then send him a bill."

She chuckled. "Sure, because you're rational and I'm emotional."

He glanced at the butcher's knife in her hand pointed at his chest. "Right now, yes."

Myaisha stuck the knife into the carving board. It stood up on end. She crossed her arms over her heaving chest and glared.

AJ climbed off the stool. "Perhaps I should leave."

She didn't move or speak. Her eyes followed AJ around the house as he gathered his coat and wallet.

He attached Zoey's leash and headed for the front door. Over his shoulder, he said, "I'll call you later."

Under her breath, Myaisha mumbled, "Yeah, you do that," while following him to the front door.

As he exited, Mrs. Lula approached.

"Hello, Mrs. Lula," AJ said, not stopping to hear her reply.

Mrs. Lula watched him enter his truck and drive off. She turned around with wrinkled brows. "Did I interrupt something?"

"No," Myaisha said, glaring at AJ's departing truck. "Perfect timing."

Half a minute passed with neither speaking. Once the trunk exited the cul-de-sac, Myaisha focused on her neighbor.

"Something wrong?"

"Oh," Mrs. Lula said, her lips trembling, "I need to ask a huge favor."

"Anything. What can I do for you?" Myaisha stepped inside the house and bumped into Boomer. "Sorry guy." She turned around. "Want to come in?"

"I can't. I…" Frowning, Mrs. Lula glanced past Myaisha and into the foyer. "It's a lot to ask, but I need to leave tomorrow."

Myaisha's left brow raised. "I hope it's nothing terrible. Did you need a ride?"

"No. I want you to watch my house—just for a few days."

"Sure," Myaisha said, observing Mrs. Lula's wrinkled brow. "But what's wrong?" She had never seen the septuagenarian distressed. *What could discombobulate Mrs. Lula?*

"It's nothing." Fishing for a key from inside her bra, Mrs. Lula handed it to Myaisha. "Would you mind? You don't have to go inside—unless I call, or you see something suspicious going on. In fact, I'd prefer you *not* go inside unless absolutely necessary."

Seconds elapsed as Myaisha studied her neighbor. Mrs. Lula generally had a mellow temperament, not prone to rash, impulsive decisions. And now she had proposed to leave—suddenly—and had asked Myaisha to watch the house but not go inside. *Didn't she understand how tempting it would be?*

"If I don't have to go inside, I won't," Myaisha promised. "Please, come in. Let's talk."

Mrs. Lula waved her off and departed. "There's a lot to do. I don't have time."

"Wait." Myaisha proceeded after her, but realized she didn't have any shoes on. By the time she slipped into sneakers, Mrs. Lula had made it to her porch. *Wow. She can move.*

Minutes passed as Myaisha gawked at Mrs. Lula's front door. Before returning inside, she glanced at Jared's house. After muttering an expletive, she shut the front door.

Chapter 5

The wide central hallway of Myaisha's medical office provided sufficient space for her to copy a school note for a patient while not impeding the staff. However, as she leaned against the wall, speaking with the child's parent, the door of exam room two flew open.

Dina burst from the room, knocking Myaisha into a small child before hurrying around the corner toward the staff restrooms.

"I'm sorry," Myaisha said, helping the child up from the floor. Once the apologies concluded, she escorted the family to the lobby. For a moment, she considered following Dina. But she had two more patients, and the office closed in an hour.

She rapped on the door of exam room two, heard "Come in," and proceeded inside.

A male patient, naked from the waist down, stood beside the exam table.

"Excuse me," Myaisha said, turning aside. "I thought you were ready."

Before she could exit, the man said, "I am."

Grimacing, Myaisha pivoted slightly, glancing at the patient. "Do you need another gown?" She spied a cloth gown on the exam table but thought it might be soiled, or the wrong size.

"Nope. I'm good."

"If you don't want to wear the gown, at least wrap it around your waist. I'll step out for a moment." She didn't wait for him to reply but closed the door. His grin seemed inappropriate, but maybe he was simply in a good mood.

A half minute elapsed before she again entered the exam room. This time, the patient sat on the exam table but remained completely exposed from the waist down.

Myaisha walked over to the sink and washed, then dried her hands. "Sir, did you not understand about wearing the gown?"

After donning gloves, she removed a paper drape from under the sink and covered the man's genitalia.

"I thought it would be easier this way."

His chipper, toothy smile made Myaisha closely scrutinize his countenance. He was a new patient, and though she had no familiarity with his behavior, Myaisha detected something odd. Remembering she expected a call from the lawyer about Jared and the fence, she pushed it aside.

"We want patients to be comfortable," she said, stepping away from the exam table.

"Oh, I'm comfortable." He winked at her.

Creep. Myaisha rested on a stool and pulled up the patient chart in the EHR, the electronic health record.

"So, Mr. Hopper. What concerns do you have today?" While asking questions, Myaisha scanned the chart. Dina listed the complaint as groin pain. *Great.*

"Well, you see, it hurts here." He pointed to his inguinal area.

Myaisha jumped off the stool. "Please remain covered."

But Mr. Hopper had ripped off the dressing, exposing his genitalia. "Come, take a look." His smirk resembled a hyena's. "Touch me all you want."

Through gritted teeth, Myaisha hissed, "Get dressed and get out. Now!"

"Wait, don't you—"

She didn't hear the rest of his comment because she slammed the exam room door. Myaisha rested against the wall across from the exam room. *How long should she give him to leave?*

Two minutes later, the door opened, and Mr. Hopper stormed out. Though he turned as if heading for the lobby, he reared back and leered in her face. "I didn't know lesbians worked in this office."

At a safe distance, Myaisha followed him into the lobby. At the picture window looking out toward the front parking lot, she watched him enter a car and drive away. Glancing around the empty lobby, she headed for the registration desk.

"If he comes back, call me—*immediately.*"

Twenty minutes later, Myaisha dismissed the last patient. In the background a vacuum hummed. She stretched her back and ambled toward the nursing triage area where Dina logged immunizations on the computer.

"May I speak with you?" she asked.

With a simple nod, Dina abandoned the computer and faced her.

"Did Mr. Hopper..." She didn't want to ask a leading question but needed to get a clear picture of what occurred. "Tell me what happened with Mr. Hopper."

Flushed, the nurse gazed at the wall then her feet.

Myaisha inched closer and lowered her voice. "Let's speak in my office."

Half a minute later, they faced each other across Myaisha's desk. Instead of questioning Dina, she waited.

Fumbling with the gloves on her hands, Dina looked up. "He dropped his pants."

"While you were in the room?"

"Yes. I was completing the intake form when he…" Dina bit her lip. Tears flooded her eyes.

Though she wanted to hug Dina, Myaisha remained respectful of her nurse's personal space. It had taken years, but therapy and patience had allowed Dina to become comfortable in the office. At least Myaisha had believed that to be true before she'd overheard Alma's and Shirley's taunts.

Another minute passed before Dina said, "I gave him a gown and told him I would leave while he undressed. But he grabbed my hand and put it…"

Myaisha wanted to help—relieve this trauma as much as possible—but she had to hear it directly from Dina.

A lone tear slid down Dina's cheek. "I ran."

With a sigh, Myaisha shoulders sunk. This office had been her dream. A medical sanctuary where she could treat patients the way she wanted, hiring staff who represented and reflected her ideas.

First, she had witnessed two of her staff behaving like bullies. Now, a sexual predator had assaulted her nurse. Myaisha's chest pounded. She started to speak but choked. Between the office, Jared, almost loosing Boomer, and Josiah not coming home…

Stay in control. This is your domain.

After clearing her throat, she said, "This will not be tolerated. Mr. Hopper will be dismissed *today*. We need to call the police—"

"No!" Dina shouted, vaulting from the chair. "Forget it."

"This isn't the first time he's done something like this. He committed a crime, violated—"

"I won't. Can't you simply remove him as a patient?"

"Yes, but he'll continue doing this to other women."

"That's not my problem. I can't speak to the police about..." She rose, fumbling with the gloves again, apparently searching for words while circling the area in front of the desk. "Not again. I don't want to talk about this. Never again." Dina wrenched the door open and fled.

At a slower pace, Myaisha followed, but Dina locked herself inside the staff bathroom. Gradually, vacuuming ceased. Alma and Shirley peeked down the hallway from the lobby. Yvette's head poked outside her office door, which was beside Myaisha's.

Gently, Myaisha knocked on the bathroom door. Her attempts to have Dina continue their conversation were met with silence. After a few minutes, she retired to her office.

***

A quarter of an hour later, the medical assistants had departed.

Unable to get Dina out of the bathroom, Myaisha had joined Yvette in the front reception area.

"What are you doing?" Myaisha asked, resting her elbows on the countertop.

"Scheduling." Yvette stopped typing and glanced up. "Now, what's going on with Dina?"

She frowned. "What do you mean?"

"I figured she was having another one of her episodes," Yvette said while typing.

"I don't understand your attitude."

"You have to admit, Mrs. Doctor, she is odd."

"She's ill," Myaisha said, massaging her neck. "Whether physical or mental, illness affects people's behavior differently." Frustrated with her staff and furious with her inability to control her world—office and home—Myaisha slammed the desktop.

How has she lost control? Why are things changing, and in such a negative way?

Noticing the office manager's searching gaze, she hurriedly said, "A patient assaulted Dina today."

Yvette gaped. "When? Who?"

Several minutes passed as she explained what had occurred. During their conversation, Myaisha heard the staff bathroom door open.

"Send Mr. Hopper a dismissal letter. I need to contact the medical board about what actions to take."

"But if Dina won't report it."

"I'll speak with her. Send the letter, today." Myaisha checked her watch. "Or first thing tomorrow. Make sure it's certified—or registered."

"Absolutely." Yvette scribbled notes on a legal pad.

Myaisha walked down the hall at the same moment Dina retrieved a handbag from under a counter in the nursing triage room.

"We need to talk."

"I have to go."

She reached forward and touched the edge of Dina's coat. "I won't push, but if you want to talk, please call me."

Dina nodded.

"If you need time off, let me know."

With a brief nod, Dina escaped out the rear office door.

Myaisha sauntered into her office and collapsed in the desk chair. She'd flubbed this big time. There weren't a lot of opportunities to practice how to speak with your staff when they're assaulted by a patient. *Do better next time.*

The rear office door closed again. She swiveled around in the chair and watched Yvette drive off. She slipped out of her Birkenstock and into dress shoes. Over the next fifteen minutes, she sauntered around the medical building. She considered the wallpaper, the furniture. Certain items she had picked out, others came from Sammy's medical office after his stroke.

Though over a decade had passed since her husband died, during the holidays his absence hurt more acutely. Christmastime represented family. Her parents and siblings all lived in California. She had moved to North Carolina with Sammy. They had purchased their home together. Once he died, she and Josiah continued to live in that same home. Now, with him gone…

But she had made a life with Josiah after her husband's death. She had developed friendships and had crafted a successful career.

Why did Sammy's absence bother her so much this year? Because Josiah was in college, and she remained alone in the house with Boomer. During the holidays her son would return, filling their family home with joy.

With a deep sigh, Myaisha gathered her purse and coat. Once all the lights in the office were extinguished, she set the alarm and left.

***

Streets whizzed by as Myaisha drove. *Has she focused more on patient care and neglected her staff?*

Perhaps she had poor judgment when it came to people. Half her mind considered her medical practice, the other reviewed her earlier conversation with the lawyer.

Myaisha's lawyer had mentioned she needed proof that Jared's kids had damaged the fence, otherwise a successful lawsuit would be unlikely. After detailing the costs of litigation, the lawyer recommended she forget about suing, simply repair the fence and install cameras around the yard.

Her shoulders sagged. She shouldn't have to pay for Jared's delinquent kids, nor surrender her privacy to Big Brother's prying eyes.

Turning left into the cul-de-sac, Myaisha's eyes widened. A trail of police vehicles and an ambulance were parked along the street. Neighbors dotted the sidewalk. She scanned the area, searching for Boomer but couldn't find him anywhere.

CHAPTER 6

Gripping the steering wheel, Myaisha sped into her driveway. Sweat dripped down her spine. The engine barely stopped before she leaped out of the car and ran toward the side fence. The boards were intact, exactly as AJ had installed them yesterday evening.

AJ. She had been obstinate. He had simply wanted to protect Boomer—and her. *Should she call him?* Later. Right now, she needed to discover why the police were parked in front of Jared's house.

Since the fence remained intact, Myaisha scanned the crowd hovered at the foot of Jared's driveway. "What happened?" she asked, hurrying over to Roger.

"Humph," Roger mumbled, rolling the pipe tip around mouth. "Not sure." His gaze fastened on the front door. "According to Mrs. Allen, Patsy came running outside screaming her head off like a banshee. I was stringing Christmas lights up around the garage door when I heard the sirens. Almost fell off the ladder."

How long is he going to wander from the question?

"What happened?" she asked again, stepping forward slightly obstructing his view.

"Oh, I'm not sure. I told Abigail to call the police, but they were already pulling up."

She frowned. "Who called them?"

"No idea, little lady. I suppose…"

Noticing Mrs. Lula headed their direction, Myaisha abandoned Roger to his rubbernecking.

"Mrs. Lula, are you—"

"I need to leave. Can you still watch my place?" the septuagenarian asked, breathing heavily.

Myaisha noticed Mrs. Lula's side glance at Jared's house. Otherwise, she seemed disinterested in the police activity. *What's going on?*

"Yes, of course." She laid a hand on Mrs. Lula's shoulder. Her fingers bumped against a strap. Bra— awfully thick though. *What else could it be?*

Myaisha recalled the tutorial Grace, her private eye friend, had given the Greensboro Women of Color Writing Group last month. A gun holster. She scrutinized her neighbor. "If you're in trouble, I can help."

"You are helping, child. Thank you." Mrs. Lula moved away but not before a uniformed police officer joined them.

"Ma'am," he said, addressing Mrs. Lula, "the detectives want to speak with you again."

"Then they better hurry up. I got things to do." She checked a large wind-up watch on her wrist, tightening the coat around her neck. "It's cold as a witch's titty out here. Y'all have me catching pneumonia."

"Would you like to wait inside my house?" Myaisha asked, wanting to delay Mrs. Lula's departure, giving them an opportunity to talk.

"I want to be about my business." The senior citizen clapped her lips shut and pouted at the police officer.

Lanky Detective Todd Gamble, wearing a plush, long coat, hurried over. "Mrs. Lula, I'm sorry to keep you waiting."

Crossing her arms over her chest, Mrs. Lula glared at the detective. "Well, you should be. I'm too old for this, and it's freezing out here." She pointed a gloved hand at the uniform officer. "That dull-looking young man said you needed to talk to me again. 'Bout what?"

Todd side-eyed Myaisha, who retreated a foot.

She could already hear Todd's complaint about her interference. But this time, she had a genuine reason to be concerned—especially now that the situation involved a homicide detective. *But who had been murdered?*

If Patsy murdered Jared, Myaisha would happily testify in defense of the abused wife. True, she had never seen Jared *physically* strike Patsy. His demeaning comments and verbal assaults were enough. Though Myaisha encouraged her to leave, Patsy incessantly proclaimed Jared's love and commitment to their family.

Patsy could've snapped. Between Jared's bullying and those obnoxious kids…

From her yard, Myaisha watched the paramedics carry a body draped in a thick gray sheet from the house. Despite straining, she couldn't make out any distinctive features.

Did Jared finally drink himself to death, or did someone help him along? If the former, their cul-de-sac might host a party. Most people in their tiny neighborhood had little affection for Jared. It hadn't always been that way. *When did things change?*

While considering how her neighbor had changed over the years, Myaisha looked inside her neighbor's front window. She observed Patsy moving around the kitchen. *Is that where Jared had died?* If Todd had been assigned the case, it had to be a homicide.

She exhaled and relaxed, rubbing her neck. As a smile crept across her face, Myaisha startled. *Am I actually happy Jared died?* Ghoulish and uncharitable but true. *Did I dislike him that much?*

Chastened, her attention left Patsy and focused on Todd's interview with Mrs. Lula.

"I want to clarify the information about the delivery van," Todd said, shivering.

"What about it?" Mrs. Lula said, conspicuously jiggling her keys.

Myaisha suppressed a grin, aware of her neighbor's deliberate attempt to hurry Todd along.

"You're sure the delivery truck—"

"Brown, four wheels, yellow signage on the side. I'm old, young man, not stupid—or blind."

The detective's chin tensed. "Anything else."

Mrs. Lula frowned. "Nope. Don't remember anything other than what I already told ya."

"Yes, ma'am. Thank you."

As Todd closed his book, Mrs. Lula departed. "We'll contact you if we have further questions."

"Good luck with that."

The whistling wind obscured much of Mrs. Lula's final comment. Myaisha doubted Todd heard it. She heard it because she had started to follow Mrs. Lula. But hearing someone calling her name, Myaisha stopped and swiveled around.

"Oh, Myaisha, I'm so glad you're home." Patsy embraced her and squeezed tightly. "This has been a nightmare."

Smeared mascara testified to Patsy's sorrow. She had no coat on and shuddered in Myaisha's arms.

"You need to go inside."

"I can't." Patsy's head and body shook. "Not in there. He… I found him on the floor." Her face paled, and her enormous blue eyes widened.

Afraid Patsy might faint, Myaisha supported her by the arm. "Come inside with me."

"Wait." Patsy squiggled out of her grip. "My kids. Can they come too?"

Myaisha wavered, perhaps longer than considered polite. Although she wanted to console Patsy and offer support, she didn't care for Patsy's children. They were disobedient and rude. Besides, they'd burned her fence, which was how Boomer got out of the yard, and Jared had threatened to have him put down.

Seconds elapsed—almost a minute—before Myaisha consented. "Go get them. I'll be inside."

***

In the minutes before Patsy and the kids arrived, Myaisha had let Boomer outside. Last night, she had disconnected the automatic doggie door. She didn't want her Lab in the yard when she wasn't home. Jared had made it clear that if Boomer got outside again…

Well, she didn't have to worry about him anymore. *Jerk got what he deserved.* A pang of guilt stabbed Myaisha's chest. She reflected on her attitude. The doorbell rang and she shook off the thought.

"Thanks for letting us stay," Patsy said, herding her brood inside.

As each kid entered, Myaisha gave them a stern warning glance. All three children sulked and crashed on the living room couch that faced the backyard.

Patsy joined the children, hugging them to her side. "Dr. Douglas has been very kind. What do you say?"

The kids regarded Myaisha for a moment with indifference, then looked elsewhere.

"What do we say?" Patsy repeated, grasping the children's faces, forcing them to look at her.

"Thank you," they said, mockingly.

With a sigh, Patsy sank against the couch pillows. "Very good."

Yeah, right. Myaisha eyed the children, letting them know she understood what they were about.

"Why don't you guys go find something to play with in Josiah's room?" Patsy said. "I'm sure he left toys or games around. You don't mind do you, Myaisha?"

"Actually," she hurried into the living room, "the games are here. Josiah doesn't like people in his room." *Especially demons on two legs.*

She removed several games from the cabinets beside the fireplace. The children rushed to retrieve them and were soon playing a board game.

"Would you like something to drink—tea or hot chocolate?" Myaisha asked Patsy.

But the children answered first. "Hot chocolate."

One boy said, "I'm hungry."

"When are we gonna eat, Mama?" the little girl asked.

Myaisha removed a bag of fries and some frozen turkey burgers from the refrigerator. From the pantry, she opened a bag of pretzels and poured them into a large bowl. She placed them on the floor beside the children.

In a low voice, she said, "And don't make a mess."

When the boy made a face and reached for the bowl, she pulled it away.

"I. Mean. It." Her gaze zeroed in on him before she released the bowl.

With a whistle, Boomer bounded to her side. "Watch them."

Boomer sat at attention at the head of the hallway, blocking the path to Josiah's bedroom.

In the kitchen, Myaisha prepared a salad while the turkey burgers defrosted in the microwave.

"Sorry about this," Patsy said, taking a seat on a stool at the kitchen island. "I couldn't go inside—not with all those police officers."

Chewing on her bottom lip, Patsy gazed at the far wall. "Besides, it was chilly with the door opening all the time. Cops coming and going. And the kids were getting in the officers' way."

"Why didn't you go stay with Roger and Abigail? He would've loved the company."

Patsy shook her head. "She's an invalid. The kids drive her crazy."

Multiple sclerosis isn't the reason those kids bother her.

"Tiffany and Carter would've let you in."

Patsy accepted the tea. She palmed the cup in her hand, inhaling the steam without drinking. "I didn't want to be a bother."

But you'll burden me with your brats.

Crash!

Boomer barked.

Myaisha hurried to the entertainment center.

"Sorry," the girl said, looking sourly at a book sprawled on the floor for a second before running off with her brothers.

After checking the shelving, Myaisha returned the book to a higher location. "No problem. Nothing's broken." *This time.*

She shuffled the children into the kitchen nook beside a large bay window overlooking the backyard. "Sit here. Dinner's about ready."

"But we weren't done playing," one boy whined.

"Well, you are now."

The other asked, "When is daddy coming back from the hospital?"

"I'm not sure," Patsy said.

Mugs of hot chocolate were deposited on the table before Myaisha returned to prepare dinner. Boomer trotted into the kitchen, eyeing the kids.

As she dropped a handful of French fries into crackling hot oil, Myaisha asked, "So, what happened?"

"I don't know," Patsy said, gazing absently into an empty mug and chewing on her bottom lip.

Myaisha took the mug from her and refilled it with tea. "Why are…" her voice lowered, "homicide detectives there?"

"Probably because the paramedics couldn't explain what happened. I thought Jared had a seizure."

She frowned. "I didn't know he had a seizure disorder."

"Neither did I," Patsy muttered distantly. "But why else would he collapse and die?"

Studying Patsy's face, Myaisha considered whether the absent, vacant gaze represented sorrow, amazement, or confusion.

"Tell me—"

Knock, knock.

Myaisha got up and answered the door. Boomer, however, remained beside the table watching the kids.

Todd stood on her doorstep. "I'm looking for Mrs. Lowery."

"Come in. She's in the kitchen. I'm making dinner for the kids."

He followed behind her, surveying the floors.

She smiled. "Boomer's in the kitchen, watching the kids."

"Mrs. Lowry," Todd said, his eyes immediately fastening on the Lab, "I wanted to let you know we're leaving. The officers called us in because they found no identifiable cause of death, but that doesn't mean…" He hesitated.

Myaisha followed his gaze to the children sitting in the nook. She removed the fries from the stove, added salt, and served them on a rectangular plate.

"Here guys," she said, addressing the children. "Burgers up in another minute."

They grabbed at the hot dish, pushing each other aside. While the children devoured the food, Myaisha walked over to Todd.

In a low voice, he said, "We don't know if your husband died from *interference*." He raised his eyebrows suggestively. "Once the medical examiner lets me know what occurred, I'll contact you."

Patsy managed a tiny smile. "Thank you, detective."

"Here's my card." A rectangular manila card flicked between Todd's thin, long fingers. "Call if you remember anything that might help. We've cleared out. You can return home whenever you're ready."

"Really?" Like a Jack-in-the-box, Patsy leaped off the kitchen island stool. "Oh, that's wonderful." She rushed over to the children. "Come on guys, we can leave."

With a spatula in her hand, Myaisha asked, "But what about the burgers?"

"Thanks, but we'd rather eat at home." Patsy touched her shoulder. "And I really appreciate everything you did." In an instant, she pivoted toward her kids. "Let's go. *Now.*"

Chairs scraped along the wooden floors as three children jumped from their seats and followed after their mom. Fries were strewn across the table and floor. The children hustled behind Patsy and out the front door. Boomer followed and remained at the door as Myaisha secured the lock.

She returned to the kitchen shaking her head. "Lord, give me patience."

Boomer ate fries off the floor, licking up any remnants.

Burgers sizzled in the frying pan. "You hungry?" she asked Todd.

"Sure."

"The bathroom is down the hall."

As Todd left, she glanced down at Boomer. "You want a burger with those fries?"

Woof.

By the time Todd returned, Myaisha had cleared away the dishes Patsy's kids had left and had a plate of fries and a burger ready.

Boomer briefly lifted his head and growled at Todd, then quickly returned to consuming his meal.

"Lemonade or tea?"

He grinned. "You have to ask?"

In under a minute, she placed a frosty glass of lemonade on the table.

She sat across from him. "So, are you going to tell me what happened?"

"I have no idea."

Neither spoke as they consumed their meals. Boomer sauntered over to the table, lying his head on her leg.

"You finished your burger, and now you want mine?"

Woof. His large dark eyes drooped.

She considered her expanding waistline a moment before saying, "Fine." After placing her remaining burger in his food bowl, she prepared more tea and rejoined Todd at the table.

"Who called you?"

"The first officer on the scene. Apparently, the wife came home, found her dead husband, and called 911."

"Did you mean what you said to Patsy, you don't know the cause of death?"

He nodded. "Right now, the most likely cause is poison—assuming it wasn't a natural death. The paramedics reported no bruises or other signs of trauma to his body."

"Well, if anyone on this street deserved to be murdered, Jared fit the bill. Surprised he hadn't been killed before now."

"So, I understand."

She scrutinized him. "What've you heard?"

Todd continued to eat. Taking his time, he wiped his mouth and set his napkin aside. Gazing deeply into her wide eyes, he said, "I've been told you had a great motive."

CHAPTER 7

Todd left after consuming two turkey burgers. After he departed, Myaisha stood on the porch and glanced around the neighborhood. All the police vehicles had disappeared. The inhabitants of her cul-de-sac had returned to their homes. Despite the cold night, she remained outside, observing Patsy's home.

Though the entryway light flickered off through parted curtain windows, Myaisha spied inside the kitchen. The children gathered around Patsy at the stove.

Where had Jared been killed?

Todd had only spoken in generalities. Officially, Jared's death hadn't been classified as a homicide. Myaisha had never seen Jared ill, nor had Patsy ever mentioned him suffering from any medical condition. In fact, Patsy had acted surprised by Jared's sudden death.

Shaking away her suspicions, Myaisha returned inside. Mystery writers conjured up a dozen different ways to kill people. Sometimes a person simply died, an unfortunate fact of life.

Still, Jared made a perfect murder victim. Arrogant, rude, and boisterous. Myaisha imagined few people in the neighborhood would mourn his death.

While cleaning dishes at the sink, her cellphone rang. She peeked at the screen.

Josiah.

Without drying her hands, she pressed the answer button.

"Hi, guy," she said.

"Hey Mom. How're things?"

"Fine. Well, at least for me." She dried her hands. "How did exams go?"

"All right, I guess. I won't get the scores back for another week."

"I'm sure you did fine. Have you changed your mind about Christmas?"

His momentary silence made her stomach lurch. Boomer rested on her feet.

"Josiah?"

"No, Mom. In fact, I called to make sure you're okay. I know how much Christmas means to you."

Her bottom lip trembled. *To us. Christmas matters to us. Or had the holiday celebrations simply been about her priorities?*

Myaisha tried not to be an overbearing mother. She understood Josiah wanted—required—independence. As her only child, they had always maintained a close bond. They didn't simply do mother-son things. They did people things together—movies, roller skating, museums. She thought he considered her a friend. Now, during one of the few special events they typically enjoyed together, he didn't want to participate.

Half a minute passed with neither speaking.

She wiped tears from her eyes and cleared her throat. "I'll miss you, but it's okay if you want to be with your friends."

"Actually, I wanted to stay on campus and relax. The semester was difficult."

"Sure. Whatever you decide is fine with me."

"Thanks Mom."

"I love you."

"Love you too," Josiah said before hanging up.

Myaisha tossed the phone aside and slumped over to the couch. No Josiah for Christmas.

A half hour passed with her sitting there, absorbing this new truth. *Does she make Christmas a bigger deal than necessary?* She thought Josiah appreciated the holiday as much as she did.

Josiah would eventually have his own family. He might move away from Greensboro permanently—maybe out of North Carolina. After all, she had moved across the country and away from her family for her husband's career. Josiah might do the same. She rubbed her chest, unsure if the pain came from heartburn or heartache.

She selected an LP and placed it on the record player. *Easy* by the Commodores crooned from the speakers as she reluctantly returned to cleaning the kitchen.

Later, as she trudged into her bedroom, Myaisha considered calling AJ. She could accept his invitation to spend the holiday with his family. Slowly, a thought coalesced in her mind. Myaisha attempted to push it aside, but it persisted.

Truthfully, she didn't want to spend Christmas with AJ's family. *Why not?*

CHAPTER 8

Inside the detectives' office coffee and staleness clung to the air like funk from highway roadkill. Todd's nose wrinkled. He needed fresh air but wanted to complete this last report. As he typed the last word, his partner, Detective Ian De Jesus entered.

The elongated rectangular office space contained over a dozen separate desks. Todd and Ian had positioned theirs to face each other.

Dropping a brown bag on his desk, Ian draped a suit coat over the back of the chair and sat. "Morning."

Todd grunted.

"That good, huh?" Ian opened the brown bag and bit into a sandwich. "Anything on that recent death in East Greensboro?"

"Not yet," Todd said, checking his report for errors. "The medical examiner said she'd call if—"

The desk phone rang.

"Yeah," Todd said, answering the phone while still reviewing his report while the person on the other end of the line spoke. Intermittently, he jotted notes on a legal pad. "So, it looks like poison, but you haven't identified it yet?"

A minute passed before he ended the call.

"Tell me," Ian asked, sipping coffee from a paper cup.

"The body showed signs of poisoning, but no ID on the source."

Ian squinted, reviewing his notepad. "I remember something about a bottle." For a moment, the only sounds came from him turning pages.

"A water bottle?" Todd asked, typing the information forensics had provided into his report.

"Got it." Ian slid his notepad across their desks to Todd. "Beer bottle."

"I see." Todd rubbed his forehead. "How did forensics miss that?" He returned the notepad.

"They didn't." Ian guzzled the remaining coffee. "You were talking to the medical examiner. The bottle would be with the lab. I'll call them." He picked up the desk phone and dialed.

***

When Todd returned to his desk after a short stop at the vending machine, Ian was still on the phone.

"I simply want to know if you've got anything?" Ian asked, making an exasperated face at Todd.

"Fine. I'll check back later." Ian started to hang up the phone.

"And don't call again until tomorrow," a voice shouted over the phone.

"Okay." He slammed down the receiver.

Smirking, Todd said, "I presume they have nothing."

"Those guys in the lab have major attitude. Told me not to call before Monday."

"Monday. We need to wrap this up before Christmas."

"We may not be able to."

"Without knowing the cause of death…" Todd gazed over his partner's shoulder at a calendar hanging on the far wall.

"It's poison. We start there."

Though he had heard Ian, Todd didn't reply. He busily counted the days until—

"You worried about your recital?"

"It's not a recital."

"Whatever." Ian wolfed down the rest of his breakfast sandwich and tossed the wrapper in the trash. "You'll do fine."

"Are you coming?" he asked, tearing his focus away from the calendar.

"Wouldn't miss it." Ian wiped his hands on a napkin before typing. "I think you should invite the department. Some refined culture would be good for these bone heads."

"I don't believe the team would appreciate a violin concerto."

Ian shrugged. "You don't know. Cops appreciate music."

"Eighteenth century composers? I've never heard Bach blasting in the parking lot or crooning from anyone's music player."

"Maybe they're embarrassed to show they appreciate classical music—like you."

"I'm not embarrassed."

"Then why won't you invite the entire department?"

"Because I invited people who matter to me."

"Whatever." Ian opened his notepad. "Where do we start with the interviews?"

"Let's leave the wife for last," Todd said. "She's got her hands full with the kids and notifying relatives."

"The neighbors then. Which first?" Ian rose and slid into his suit coat.

"I already spoke with Myaisha Douglas."

"What?" Ian gaped. "Her again."

Todd glared at his partner. "Don't start."

"Why is your girlfriend always involved in our homicides?"

Slipping into gloves, Todd said, "First, she is not my girlfriend. Second, you exaggerate. She is not involved in *all* our cases."

"Enough to be a pain in the—"

"Watch it."

"Dude, you seriously like her."

Todd ignored the comment and departed with Ian at his side.

"Come on. Be honest."

Though he detected the heat from Ian's scrutiny, Todd avoided his partner's gaze. "It's not like that."

"What is it then?" Ian said, bustling out the station door before him.

How would I describe my relationship with Myaisha?

A friend, but more. Confidante, no. She also irritated him, but…

From the passenger seat, Ian unwrapped a candy bar. "Why aren't we moving?"

Sending a terse glance at his partner, Todd started the engine and exited the police parking lot.

CHAPTER 9

As his partner trod up to the front door, Todd surveyed the neighborhood. Nothing looked unusual or out of place. Slightly over half the homes displayed holiday decorations. Once he had considered each house in the cul-de-sac, his gaze meandered over to Myaisha's.

Given her proximity to the deceased's home—not to mention her dispute regarding the fence and the dog—Todd had to acknowledge her as a suspect. Until he gathered more information about the crime, however, he would not treat her as such.

Boom, boom, boom.

He flinched. "Ian, take it easy."

"You're the one who changed his mind about interviewing her."

"Until we know differently, she's a victim—the deceased's wife."

His partner shrugged. "Most people are murdered by their nearest and dearest."

"All I'm saying is don't break down the door."

"I make no promises." Ian smirked as the front door creaked open.

"Good morning, Mrs. Lowry," Todd said, displaying his official homicide detective badge. "I don't know if you remember me and my partner, Detective de Jesus."

Her wide, clear, dry eyes blinked rapidly, reminding Todd of a moth flickering around a light bulb.

"Umm, not really," she said, chewing her bottom lip.

Todd lifted his badge slightly. "I'm Detective Gamble. We wanted to update you on our investigation."

Mrs. Lowry remained frozen on the doorstep. Todd wondered if she could be in shock or simply didn't want to talk.

"We could come back later—"

"Oh, that would be great," she said, starting to close the door.

"But this is important," he said, slipping his foot across the threshold.

Though she stopped shutting the door, Mrs. Lowry still didn't invite them inside.

Coming up beside him, Ian said, "We wanted to give you an update. You must be concerned about what caused your husband's death."

"Of course." Mrs. Lowry spoke absently, gathering a red and green checkered robe around her chest. "Did you find out what happened?"

Frustrated, and cold, Todd asked, "May we come in? It's windy today."

Mrs. Lowry's brow furrowed. "I suppose. It's just that..."

"It won't take long."

As she stepped aside, Todd scanned the hallway and distant living room. Debris cluttered the ground, making it difficult to discern the actual flooring.

He smiled. "We understand how things are with children."

Her countenance lifted. "Thank you." Finally, she bade them enter. "Please, come in. They're good kids—usually."

She closed the door behind Ian. "It's just that a lot has happened since yesterday. I haven't had a chance to clean up."

"We understand," Todd said as he approached the living room, carefully avoiding toy army men scattered along the floor. These were the children who, according to Myaisha, set fire to a fence with matches and fireworks—not his idea of good kids.

Ian entered the living room and sat on a chair beside an old-fashioned brick fireplace with a foot-high stack of natural wood logs. Floor-to-ceiling cabinets hugged both sides of the fireplace, crowded with books, toys, and bric-a-brac. While his partner took notes, Todd sat on the couch next to Mrs. Lowry.

"What have you told the children?" Todd asked, noticing her gaze resting on the fireplace.

"Nothing," she said distantly. "I mean—I told them their dad became sick and had to go to the hospital."

Todd nodded.

"It wasn't really a lie," she said, lowering her eyes to the carpet.

"No, it wasn't."

She tightened the robe's drawstring, clutching the fabric up around her neck. As her eyes widened, Mrs. Lowry leaned forward, almost onto his lap. "So, what actually happened? Did Jared have a seizure? Probably from drinking all that beer."

Sitting up straighter, Todd said, "The medical examiner confirmed your husband died from poisoning."

"What!" Mrs. Lowry practically leaped from the couch. "How? From where?"

Rising also, Todd said, "We haven't identified the actual poison."

"Poison." Her gaze wandered around the room before returning to the fireplace. Mumbling, Mrs. Lowry said, "Something he ate or drank."

Half a minute passed before she shrieked, "The food!" Hurrying into the kitchen, Mrs. Lowry began opening cabinets. "What did Jared eat yesterday? What if the kids…"

"Ma'am…"

She ran back and grasped Todd's arm. "Should I take the children to the hospital?"

Todd assisted her to a chair at the square kitchen table. "Right now, the forensic lab hasn't identified the source. Yesterday they picked up a beer bottle lying beside your husband's hand. With your permission, we would like to sample other food items and beverages in the house."

"Yes, please," Mrs. Lowry said, gnawing on her lip. "When?"

Ian slightly inclined his head. "They're outside now."

"Oh." Mrs. Lowry frowned. She glanced up at Todd, then beyond him into the living room.

Without turning around, Todd knew for certain she was looking at the fireplace. *But why?*

Maybe the stockings along the mantel made her think about family and her now deceased husband. She might be cold and considering starting a fire. Or, more likely, something on the fireplace—or cabinets—contained an item of interest. She looked worried. *What could it be?*

As a homicide detective, Todd's interest had been piqued. He needed to figure out what item concerned Mrs. Lowry, especially since the case had morphed into a homicide investigation—probably.

As his partner had said, most people died at the hands of their closest relatives. Mrs. Lowry instantly became the prime suspect in her husband's death. Right now, though, Todd simply wanted to search the fireplace and cabinets. However, they had no probable cause.

The medical examiner stated the deceased had been poisoned, but until they identified the substance Mr. Lowry's death might have been accidental. He needed to check with the chief. It served no purpose to search the home if a judge deemed it illegal and tossed out all the evidence they uncovered. He'd get permission first. Hopefully, whatever Mrs. Lowry had hidden wouldn't be destroyed before he obtained a warrant.

While Ian left to inform the forensics team they had permission to enter, Mrs. Lowry frantically picked up toys and other items off the floor. Todd, in a pretense of helping, cleared the area near the fireplace.

"Give me a minute," Mrs. Lowry said. "I'll grab the children's toy box. It'll make things easier."

In her absence, Todd scanned the fireplace and surrounding cabinets. Surruptiously, he snapped photos. At least if they came back later with a warrant, he would know if anything had been moved.

Dressed in white jumpsuits, face masks, and goggles, three individuals from forensics entered the kitchen and removed items from the refrigerator and cabinets. Todd allowed Ian to observe their work. Determined to discover what about the fireplace preoccupied Mrs. Lowry, Todd scanned its content from top to bottom.

CHAPTER 10

Chatter around the conference room reached a crescendo. Myaisha tried to ignore the enticing scents coming from Green Pastures Café while repeatedly checking her watch.

Each week, she held a card game at her home with her best friend, Deniece, Deniece's husband, Barry, and AJ. It took less than twenty minutes to drive from the café to her house, but the Greensboro Women of Color Writing Group's monthly meeting had not ended yet. Concerned about being late, she texted Deniece.

RUNNING LATE. LET YOURSELF IN.

"Ladies, please," Tina said, straining to speak over the chatter. "We're nearly done." She nodded toward Mary seated in the front row.

"The writing conference," Mary said.

"Right." Tina wiped perspiration from her forehead. "We need to collect the money for the writing conference next Spring in Tennessee. You have to pay by Tuesday to take advantage of the early registration discount."

Gradually, rumblings around the room increased again.

Mary rose and joined Tina. "If you aren't sure, contact me or Tina during the week. We'll accept check or cash—no IOUs," she added with a stern expression.

"That's it for our December meeting. The Greensboro Women of Color Writing Group will meet again in January…" Before Tina could share any more departing words, people began abandoning their seats and heading for the exit in the rear.

Once the door leading to the café opened, Myaisha inhaled the delicious smells of fried food and sugary treats. Her stomach grumbled, but she remembered the weekly game of spades—not to mention the additional weight she had acquired since Thanksgiving.

Deniece and Barry would bring dinner—at least it was their turn. *Should I call and remind them?*

She could bring snacks for the group, in case they forgot. No one would object to extra food. Pinching from her too-tight waistband made her reconsider. At worst, Boomer would devour the leftovers. Myaisha detected movement beside her and moved backward.

"I'm sorry," Mary said. "Didn't mean to scare you. How are you?"

"I'd be jumpy too," Tina said, while shoving folders into a duffel bag.

Wrapping an arm around Myaisha's shoulders, Mary repeated, "How are you doing?"

"Fine. Why?"

Mary and Tina shared a look.

Tina zipped up the bag. "She means about the murder."

Myaisha looked dazed. "What murder?"

"Your neighbor," Mary said with slight exaggeration. "Have you become so accustomed to murders that one committed next door doesn't bother you?"

"Oh, him." Myaisha pulled the purse strap higher along her shoulder and took her place in line at the café register. "Yes. Too bad."

"Too bad." Mary gawked.

"Clearly you two weren't close," Tina said, smirking.

After another glance at her watch, Myaisha left the line and zigzagged between the abandoned chairs toward the exit. Deniece hadn't replied to her text. *Maybe I should call AJ.*

Mary and Tina followed, discussing the murder as they exited the café. Myaisha held onto her fedora as a sharp gust hit them. Saturdays she always wore Sammy's old fedora and didn't intend to lose it to North Carolina's weather.

"They haven't identified the poison yet?" Mary asked no one in particular, while buttoning up her coat.

Myaisha shivered as a brisk wind eddied around them. She bustled toward her car, slipping on gloves as they walked to the parking lot.

"Nope," Tina said, trotting to keep up with her.

"Who do you suspect, Myaisha?" Mary asked, pulling a fuzzy pink cap over her head.

"Don't know, don't care."

Tina snickered. "Sure. A murder is committed right next door and you're not interested."

"He hadn't been a nice neighbor." Myaisha unlocked the car door.

Standing beside her minivan, Mary said, "I heard what he did to Boomer."

Eyeballing her, Tina asked, "When? No one told me. What did he do?" Her eyes pleaded for information.

In under a minute, Mary relayed the incident regarding the fence.

"That's terrible." Tina laid a hand on Myaisha's arm. "I know you were pissed."

"You have no idea." Myaisha tossed her purse inside the Honda.

"Do the police suspect you?" Mary asked, wrapping a fluffy pink wool scarf around her neck.

"Of course not," Myaisha snapped.

"You had a motive." Mary stared in the distance counting items off on her fingertips. "Proximity to the crime and—"

"The knowledge to administer a poison," Tina said in a tone too chipper for Myaisha's taste.

Sitting in the driver's seat, Myaisha regarded her friends. *Is this what happened from reading too much crime fiction? Had we become numb to death?*

A moment passed before she said, "Nonsense. The police don't consider me a suspect."

"I'm sure Todd doesn't." Tina's grin made heat climb up Myaisha's spine.

"Oh, is he the other man?" Mary asked, cuddling conspiratorially up to Tina.

"What?" Myaisha gawked. "Todd's not—"

Ignoring her, Tina conversed with Mary. "You remember him. Tall, military crew cut, with long, delicate fingers. He plays the piano."

"The violin," Myaisha said automatically.

"Actually, he plays both," Tina said, smugly.

Mary shook her head. "Uh, uh. I don't remember him."

"Sure, you do. He interviewed you after Candace's murder." Tina stepped over a large crack in the sidewalk, coming close to Mary's side. "Real intense dark eyes."

Mary and Tina continued conversing, ignoring her protestations. Irritated by her discomfort about her friends' discussion of Todd, Myaisha waved and said her goodbyes. From the rearview mirror, she watched Mary and Tina continuing their conversation.

Did other people suspect her of being involved with Todd? Since when?

They had been spending more time together, but that was because…

Cold air from the vents made her turn up the heat. She switched on the radio, attempting to drown out her thoughts. The radio blasted *U Got It Bad* by Usher. Immediately, she flipped stations. Five minutes of public radio failed to mute her friends' accusations, so she clicked it off. Lately, she *had* been spending more time with Todd than with AJ.

If my friends believe I have feelings for Todd, what do strangers think?

Todd had a holiday violin concert and had asked her to listen to him practice. Also, they shared an interest in mysteries and criminology. AJ hated mysteries, particularly murder mysteries.

Todd enjoyed puzzles, novels, *and* chocolate. He absolutely swooned over her desserts.

They had a mutually beneficial relationship built on respect and appreciation for each other's talents, but it wasn't romantic. Simple and platonic—at least on her part.

How did Tina get the idea Todd and I were romantically involved? Had Todd said something to Ian about us?

AJ had been busy starting his new remodeling business. *Did I feel neglected?*

Aloud, she said, "Don't be ridiculous."

After Sammy died, she had spent a lot of time alone. Indeed, AJ had been her first and only relationship since her husband's death. She and Todd innocently shared mutual interests, and recently AJ had been preoccupied. *Could this be what made me push AJ away?*

There. Myaisha finally allowed herself to acknowledge the truth. She had been placing distance between herself and AJ. *Could it be from my repressed feelings for Todd?*

She shook her head. The homicide detective wasn't the type of man who appealed to her—at least not romantically or sexually. Myaisha preferred tall, athletic men her age or older.

What is happening then, if it's not another man? Why have I pushed AJ away?

Myaisha glanced at the clock dashboard and realized she would be late to their evening game of spades. She increased her speed and focused on the road.

CHAPTER 11

Lights from front porches and Christmas decorations illuminated the cul-de-sac. The garage door rose. Myaisha immediately recognized a beat-up Toyota on the right side of the garage. Elated, she flew into the house, barely avoiding a collision with Boomer. Ignoring the people seated in the kitchen nook, she rushed down the hallway toward the secondary bedrooms.

"Josiah?" she asked, opening his bedroom door.

He groggily rose from a rumpled bed. "Hey, Mom."

Myaisha sat on the side of the bed, wrapped him in a bear hug, and kissed his cheeks. Tears tottered along her eyelids.

"What time did you get home? Why didn't you call?" she asked, not giving him a moment to answer. "Are you hungry?"

Laughing, he said, "I wanted to surprise you—and I ate earlier."

Arm in arm, they entered the living room.

"Are we gonna play spades or not?" Barry asked, shuffling the cards.

Deniece smacked her husband's hand. "Be patient. Josiah's only been home from college for a few hours."

"He goes to school in Chapel Hill, not California." He dealt four hands of spades. "Mya can see him anytime."

"But I don't get to see him," Myaisha said, "because I work hard at not being an overbearing, helicopter parent."

She escorted Josiah up to AJ. "Have you two met?"

Rising from the table, AJ kissed her cheek. "Yes, Deniece introduced us." He held out a chair for Myaisha, but she declined.

"Let me prepare us a quick dinner," she said, pulling items from the refrigerator.

"Mom, I already ate. Aunt D brought me a plate of food."

Frowning, Myaisha asked her best friend, "You knew he planned to come home and didn't tell me?"

"I didn't want to ruin the surprise." Deniece grabbed Myaisha's hand, pulling her toward the table. "Come play before Barry has a fit."

"We usually play on Fridays," he huffed. "Don't see why our game has to be rescheduled to Saturday because the fool next door died."

Deniece retrieved her cards. "The neighborhood is better off without him."

"Who died?" Josiah asked, resting on the edge of a barstool.

"Mr. Lowry," Myaisha said, returning food to the refrigerator.

"Let's go," Barry said, thumping the table with his palm.

"What's your hurry?" his wife asked, the corner of her lip curling. "We always win anyways."

"Humph," Barry said, viewing his cards. "AJ and I kicked y'alls butts last month."

"Once in a blue moon," his wife said, placing a bid.

"How did he die?" Josiah asked, helping Myaisha return food to the refrigerator.

"Poison," she said, grabbing a soda before sitting down at the table.

"Probably alcohol poisoning," Josiah said. "He drank a lot."

Glancing up at him, Myaisha asked, "What do you know about his drinking?"

"Come on, Mom. I'm not a child. Anyone could recognize the signs of an alcoholic. It was common knowledge around the neighborhood."

After a quick glance at her cards, Myaisha said, "I've got nothing. Josiah, you want to play?"

"Before you and Mya started dating," Barry said, addressing AJ, "Josiah and I were partners."

"And you don't play any better with AJ," Deniece said, making a comedic face at her husband.

"No, I'm good," Josiah said. "I've got calls to make." He left the kitchen and headed for his bedroom.

"Oh, before you go," AJ said, discarding an ace of hearts and rising. "I wanted to invite you to Christmas dinner at my house. Every year my family has a huge party, with games and food. I'd like you and your mom to come."

"Thanks. Let me think about it," Josiah said before departing.

"Sure thing." Smiling, AJ resumed his seat and picked up his cards. "Nice young man."

Myaisha beamed. "Yes, but he looks thin. I wonder if he's been eating enough."

Deniece chuckled before tossing down a card. "There's nothing wrong with him. He ate the entire plate of food I brought him."

"Campus cafeteria food can be atrocious," Myaisha said, staring down the hall where her son had retreated.

"Stop worrying," Barry said, studying his hand, "and play the game."

"I don't remember you being this intense," Myaisha said, observing Barry.

"Ignore him," Deniece said. "He's in a bad mood because his office got flooded."

Myaisha asked, "When?" at the same time AJ asked, "How?"

Barry threw down his cards as Deniece tallied their scores. He clutched an empty glass of scotch. "Silly fool in the office above me had this enormous fish tank. Damn thing's been leaking for the past week. He's taking his slow sweet time getting it repaired. Destroyed a whole file cabinet of documents."

He got up and walked over to the pantry. "I need another drink."

Myaisha found the bottle, refilled his glass, and added three ice cubes. "I understand. Same thing happened with my neighbor. Six months passed, and he still hadn't fixed my fence."

"I secured the fence. Besides, he's dead," AJ said. "I thought you'd get over it by now."

Glaring at AJ, Myaisha asked, "Would you get over it, if he tried to have Zoey killed?"

The brown Lab's ears perked up. She and Boomer both looked at AJ.

"That's not what I'm saying."

Deniece rose and joined Barry on the living room couch facing the fireplace. She took a sip from his glass. "I think he's saying Jared is dead and it's over."

"Doesn't mean it didn't matter." Myaisha returned the bottle of scotch to the pantry.

"It's surprising the police aren't over here questioning you," Barry said, before swallowing his drink in one gulp. "You had motive, *and* you write murder mysteries." He held out his glass as if requesting a refill.

"You're asking for a drink after calling me a murder suspect?" Myaisha, who had entered the living room, pivoted around, and retrieved the bottle of scotch.

"I didn't say you *should* be suspected. Only I'm surprised the police *didn't* suspect you."

He raised his glass again. "Please."

"Fine."

Barry accepted the bottle and poured a healthy portion into his empty glass. "AJ?"

"I'm good." AJ reclined on the couch, inviting Myaisha to sit next to him by patting the couch cushion.

"Todd is investigating the case. He's partial to Myaisha's sweets." Deniece fluttered her eye lids and smiled suggestively.

AJ grimaced.

"Don't be silly," Myaisha said, sitting next to AJ.

He hugged her close to his side and kissed her temple. A glance at his watch made him rise and say, "It's getting late."

Deniece smacked Barry's arm. "Come on, you drunk grouch. Time to tuck you into bed."

Barry slurped the remaining scotch. "Thanks for the drink, Mya." He followed Deniece outside.

"Call you later," Deniece said, giving Myaisha a hug.

AJ leashed Zoey and headed for the foyer.

"Everything okay?" Myaisha asked, following him, and removing his coat from the foyer closet.

"Tired." He gave her a peck on the cheek. "Starting a remodeling business isn't easy. Not with also working at the station."

"That was your bright idea."

"It'll pay off in time." He gave her a short peck on the lips. "Speaking of time together, can I expect you and Josiah at my place on Christmas day?"

She shrugged. "I'll let you know."

"You said you and Josiah spend Christmas eve together. What's wrong with joining me and my family on Christmas day?"

"I said I'd think about it," she said, retreating a step.

He frowned and placed a hand on her shoulder. "What's going on?" he asked, lowering his voice.

"Nothing."

"I know we haven't had much time together with me starting this new business." He moved closer. "Are you mad at me?"

"Of course not. I'm glad you're following your dreams."

He palmed her chin in his hand. "Then what? Is it about the fence?"

"I said it's fine."

"Don't do this. If I upset you, tell me."

She paused a mere second before asking, "Why are you blaming me about the fence?"

"I'm not."

"Then why do you keep suggesting something is wrong with me?"

"Because lately you're angry all the time. I can't tell if it's something I did, or your neighbor."

"Oh, now I'm the angry Black woman?" she asked, resting her hands on her hips.

A moment passed as they stared at each other. AJ gathered the leash and exited with Zoey. A foot outside the door he spun around. "I can't fix this if you won't tell me what's wrong."

Myaisha watched him enter his double-wide truck and depart. She glanced right toward Patsy and Jared's house before returning to the living room.

***

Once everyone left, Myaisha cleaned up the kitchen. She considered speaking with Josiah about AJ's invitation but figured it could wait until tomorrow. A glance around the house revealed no Boomer. *He's probably with Josiah.*

With Boomer in Josiah's room, she had the master bedroom to herself. While braiding her hair, she considered Barry's comment.

Did the police suspect her? Should they?

On Friday, the day of the murder, Todd had come over to speak with Patsy. He hadn't interrogated Myaisha, not like he had when Candace died—likely because, at the time, he hadn't known a murder had been committed. He must have received information from the coroner's office Friday evening or Saturday to change the case to a definite murder investigation.

On Friday, would he have interrogated me if he had known a murder had been committed? Did our friendship influence his decision in considering me a homicide suspect?

When her friend, René, had been suspected of killing her twin sister, Todd's attitude toward her remained profession. He hadn't allowed their rapport to interfere with his criminal investigation. *Because of our relationship?* Possibly. He obviously valued her opinions.

Because Myaisha considered Todd a platonic friend, she hadn't worried that they hadn't openly defined their situation. *Did we have to?*

They had an innocent affection for each other. Though handsome, educated, and employed, Todd didn't romantically appeal to her. *Why not?*

Because she loved AJ. *If AJ and I weren't involved, would I be attracted to Todd?* Too many questions for a late night.

Myaisha finished braiding her hair, clicked off the lights, and climbed into bed. She didn't want answers to certain questions—not right then.

Chapter 12

Icy rain splattered Todd's face. He pulled the coat's lapel tighter around his neck frustrated at being called out on a stormy Sunday morning. Five days until the concert and he needed more practice time.

A half dozen police vehicles filled the delivery service company's visitor parking lot. Todd surveyed the area and spotted several surveillance cameras on the warehouse building.

"What are you grinning about?" Ian said, sloshing over to him along the rain-soaked asphalt.

"Cameras." Todd pointed up at the warehouse's corners. "They should come in handy."

"Hope so." Ian turned his back to the wind. "You want to come see our victim now. We'd like to get out of the rain?"

Todd followed his partner around the side of the building to the employee parking lot. After observing the surrounding area, he carefully approached the body, observing where he stepped.

The victim's upper torso lay inside a sedan, with his head resting on the driver's seat. A dried foamy substance encircled his mouth. Vomit covered his lap and the car floor. The deceased's arms stretched forward in a large V. His legs bent at the knees onto the wet ground. Todd used a handkerchief to cover his mouth as he inspected the body and car's interior.

Fifteen minutes elapsed before he retreated, allowing the forensics team to remove the corpse. He took a deep inhalation of the clean, wet air. "Identification?" he asked, headed for their department vehicle.

Flipping through his notepad, Ian gave the man's name and address.

Todd glanced around the parking lot once more. "Last seen…"

"Saturday. He completed his shift. Hung around talking to the guys. Left at seven in the evening."

He slid behind the steering wheel, waiting until Ian settled into the passenger seat to continue. "And no one noticed anything suspicious."

"Nope." Ian snapped the notebook closed and buckled up. "His wife called the boss when her husband hadn't returned home. When no one could help, she had a family member drive her out here."

As he merged behind other vehicles to depart the lot, Todd asked, "She waited all night to check up on him?"

Ian shrugged. "Maybe she thought he had an overnight shift."

"Possible."

Executing a left turn onto the main thoroughfare, Todd side-eyed Ian. "Give me her address again."

After providing the address, Ian said, "Time to interview another widow."

Chapter 13

Todd considered the murky tan fluid inside his mug. His thirst could wait but his energy could not. At five on a Monday morning, apparently no one in the police department understood how to work the coffee machine but himself. He tromped down to the staff breakroom, mentally rehearsing his violin piece. While the coffee brewed, he set aside the violin and reflected on his two new homicide cases.

The machine dinged, and Todd poured himself a cup of fresh coffee. He added creamer as the door flew open.

"There you are." Ian hurried inside, clutching a manila folder.

"Want some?"

"We're gonna need it." Ian handed Todd the folder and searched for a clean cup.

Taking a seat at one of a half dozen tables, Todd scanned the documents. "The medical examiner finished the autopsy on the delivery guy?"

"Yep." Ian sat across from Todd. "And read her conclusion."

He frowned. "Sounds like the same thing that happened to the guy in the cul-de-sac."

"That's what the M.E. thought, so she compared their tissue samples, or bodies—something like that."

Todd continued reading. "They found a bottle of water in the delivery guy's car—"

"And tested it for poison," Ian said, finishing the sentence.

Wrinkles multiplied across Todd's brow. "SMFA? Should I know what it stands for?"

"Not unless you're killing coyotes or other predators on your property."

Answering the quizzical expression on Todd's face, Ian said, "Sodium fluoroacetate."

The folder included a handout on the substance, which Todd quickly perused. "Or sodium mono-fluoroacetate, SMFA," he said under his breath.

"Pretty deadly from what the M.E. said." Ian slurped coffee. "Is there anything to eat?" He left the table in search of food while Todd continued reading.

"What does this have to do with the guy in the cul-de-sac?"

Ian returned to the table munching on a bagel. "Because they found the same stuff in his body."

As he digested the information, Todd stared at a far wall. "I remember a beer bottle near Mr. Lowry's outstretched hand, but the lab technicians didn't find any poison in it."

"Nope," Ian said, chewing on a bagel and sipping coffee. "Which means—"

"Someone planted the beer bottle."

"Clever."

"Devious." Todd's fingers tapped along the table as if playing piano keys.

Neither spoke as Ian ate and Todd read.

"According to this, SMFA has been banned in the US since 1972."

"But," Ian said before wiping his mouth, "farmers and ranchers use it to kill wolves and coyotes to protect their cattle."

"Interesting." Todd rose and poured his coffee down the sink and rinsed out the mug. "Let's go."

"Where?" Ian hustled to catch up with him.

"We need to find out which of our suspects had access to the poison."

They hurried back to their desks and started making phone calls.

Ten minutes later, Ian hung up his desk phone and started writing on a notepad. "Now we know the murders are connected, we should create a suspect list."

"Go ahead," Todd said, still on hold for the medical examiner. A minute later he hung up. "I'll try later."

"You know," Ian said, seeming to pick his words carefully, "if it's murder, we should question everyone in the cul-de-sac."

Todd shrugged. "Absolutely."

"Including the doctor."

"Who?" It took a second before Todd realized Ian's implication. "Dr. Douglas."

"She had motive."

"You can't believe—"

"And means and opportunity."

Scrutinizing his partner internally, Todd paced himself. He credited Ian as a capable, astute detective who occasionally enjoyed antagonizing him. But his partner couldn't honestly suspect Myaisha of murder.

Could he?

"Okay," he said. "What's her motive?"

"Lowry tried to kill her dog."

"No, he didn't. The victim simply called animal control when the dog got outside the fence."

"And animal control would've put him down."

"They would have investigated. Mr. Lowry hadn't been bitten. Remember, during the autopsy the medical examiner didn't locate any bruises or cuts. At most, she would have had to pay a fine and have to keep him muzzled."

"But she didn't know that."

"Of course, she did."

Ian raised his brows.

"She's capable of committing a murder, but not this one," Todd said, eyeing his partner.

"So, we should interview her?"

"We interview everybody connected with the homicide."

They both returned to their prior activities.

Minutes later, Ian said, "I contacted vendors who sell SMFA. No one reported selling the substance to any of our suspects—at least not recently, that they can remember."

"It's 2007, people can buy anything online."

"True."

Todd rose and holstered his weapon.

"Where?" Ian said, rising and putting on his coat.

"The cul-de-sac." He departed with Ian at his side. "Interview time."

"What about Dr. Douglas?"

Pressure from Ian's gaze warned Todd to tread carefully. He liked Myaisha—a lot. *Have I allowed my emotions to interfere with the investigation?*

Though passionate, she didn't possess the character of a murderer—yet how many times had he heard other people repeat the same refrain?

Ian had a point. He couldn't, shouldn't, exclude anyone. Despite their acquaintance, he had to consider her a suspect.

In truth, Myaisha made a perfect suspect. Of all the residents in the cul-de-sac, murder had become her métier.

CHAPTER 14

Todd shifted weight between his legs, stuffing his gloved hands in the plush, warm, coat pockets. "Knock again."

A minute had elapsed since the last time Ian knocked. "She's not home."

"A seventy-year-old woman has nowhere else to be on a wintry day like today."

"Well, what can I tell you. Bingo started early." Ian abandoned the front porch and headed for the next house.

A moment later Todd followed. "I don't know where Mrs. Lula can be."

At the next front door, Ian paused. "Is that her name?" Ian checked his notepad.

Todd nodded.

"What's her last name?"

Frowning, Todd realized he had no idea. He had little time to consider it further as a woman dressed in a 1980s exercise suit yelled at them from one house over.

"They're not home."

He and his partner left the house next to Mrs. Lula's and approached the shouting woman.

"Ma'am?"

She pointed at the house between hers and Mrs. Lula's. "They both work."

Leaning his head toward Todd, in a low voice Ian said, "Allen."

"Good morning, Mrs. Allen. May we speak with you a moment?"

After scrutinizing them with a heavy scowl, Mrs. Allen invited them inside.

Whatever he thought about his hostess, Todd couldn't complain about her housekeeping. The floors glistened. The 1950s furniture appeared utilitarian, though, not comforting. From the corner of his eye, Todd glimpsed a cat scamper across the floor and into the kitchen.

Accepting a seat on a firm couch facing the front door, Todd said, "We're reinterviewing neighbors."

"Figure out what killed Lowry?" she asked observing Todd's wet shoes.

"The investigation is ongoing."

"Humph," she sniffed. "Police always say that. Means you know but won't tell." Mrs. Allen shifted her narrow body along the empire chair. An electric yellow head band swept graying brown hair off her long, sloping forehead. "I could've told you he'd been murdered the first day."

Leaning forward, Ian asked, "Anything you tell us, we'll keep private."

She chuckled. "I don't care if these people know I spoke with the police. Serves them right. If you don't want people to discover your sins, don't sin." Her nose inched higher as she crossed her bony legs and reclined into the chair.

She had a point. Todd sat up straighter. "Who do you suspect?"

"Umm. My first suspect would be the doctor lady. She had motive."

Todd recoiled slightly, before reasserting his stoic demeanor. "Which doctor?"

A sinister grin formed along Mrs. Allen's mouth. "Only one doctor in this cul-de-sac, which you know very well." Her eyes twinkled.

He fought not to blush.

"Tell us," Ian said, side glancing at him.

"You should've seen her. Looked like she could've ripped Lowry in half."

"When?" Todd asked, barely finding his voice.

"Day the cops arrived. They 'bout shot her dog." Mrs. Allen snarled, "Nasty beast. Don't like anything in my house that can't bath itself."

Says the cat lady. Todd had spotted three different felines since they entered the home.

"The dog is aggressive?" he asked, tapping his fingers along the chair cushion.

"Nooo," Mrs. Allen admitted, softly. "Just who would want a hairy beast slobbering and shedding all over the place. Can't understand people with pets inside their house, unless it's a cat. Now, I grew up—"

"Did you see Dr. Douglas on the day Mr. Lowry died?" Ian asked.

Relieved Ian ended the diatribe, Todd tried to focus on the interview and not on his reaction to what Mrs. Allen had said about Myaisha.

"No. She got home after Patsy called the police. But she writes murder stories. Believes she's Patricia Cornwell. Huh. She'll never sell anything."

Turning toward Todd, she asked, "Is that why you're at her house all the time? You suspect her, or is it something else?"

"If you could focus on what happened on the day of the murder?" Todd said, too defensively to be benign.

"Don't get huffy." Mrs. Allen straightened a pillow which had fallen on its side. "Be careful. Her regular boyfriend is a firefighter. He could break your twiggy body in half." She laughed.

Noticing Ian fighting to suppress a grin, Todd's jaw twitched. "What did you see the day of the murder?"

Mrs. Allen recounted the morning of the murder from when she awoke until the police arrived. Two cats slunk into the living room, curling around her legs.

Ian balanced the notepad on his knee. "You saw a gardener?"

"Believe so." Her brow creased in thought.

"What about this gardener?" Todd asked.

Her gaze widened. "Nobody on this street employs a gardener." Mrs. Allen regarded them both in turn.

"Several witnesses reported a gardener on the street the day Mr. Lowry died, walking out the cul-de-sac and around the corner."

A tiny grin crept up Mrs. Allen's face. "I know. Interesting, isn't it?"

Todd gritted his teeth. Though she could be a valuable witness, Mrs. Allen irritated him. Not simply because of her poor fashion sensibility and cats, but her acidic appraisal of everyone and everything. Realizing she had noticed his time spent at Myaisha's house—before and since the murder—didn't improve his opinion of her. But she knew details and didn't mind sharing with the police.

Put your emotions aside and focus on her narrative. Gardener no one hired—at least according to the community busybody.

With him preoccupied, Ian said, "You mentioned other 'goings-on' in the neighborhood."

Preening, Mrs. Allen uncrossed her legs and eyed Ian. "Bed hopping, if you ask me."

"Who?"

She chuckled and the cats dispersed. "Most of them." In an aside to Todd, she said, "But not the doctor. At least she has some standards."

This time Todd knew he blushed.

Ian clicked his pen and opened his pad. "Back to the bed hopping."

Adjusting her body toward Ian, Mrs. Allen said, "The Stilwells and the Lowrys were close until…um, maybe two years ago."

"Know what happened?" Ian asked, glancing up from his notepad.

"Once, I asked Tiffany. She said their schedules changed." Mrs. Allen clicked her teeth—or dentures. "I bet they grew tired of Patsy. She's a stupid woman. Completely useless. Can't even control those deviants she conceived."

"The kids who burned Dr. Douglas's fence."

She shot Todd a glance. "So, you heard about that. The doctor was furious. Jared promised to fix her fence. Of course, he never did." Mrs. Allen relaxed against the seat cushions when a fourth cat leaped onto her lap. "That's what made your girlfriend mad."

Todd took a deep breath. "Why would one of the Stilwells want to kill Mr. Lowry?"

Regarding him as if he were daft, she said, "That's your job."

Using the notepad, Ian covered the bottom of his mouth.

"Anything else you wish to share, ma'am?" Todd said, disregarding his partner's antics.

"No," she removed a speck of lint from her pants leg. "I would think you already had enough information to discover the murderer."

Todd rose and shook her hand, avoiding the cat's paw. "Thank you for your time." He handed her a card. "Please call if you remember anything else."

She placed the card on a salver in the center of a coffee table. "I doubt there's more I can tell you—nothing associated with the murder at least."

Todd appreciated the hint in her statement but decided not to pursue it. He had no interest in gossip unassociated with the homicide. Besides, Mrs. Allen might mention something about his time spent at Myaisha's. He knew Ian would bring up his involvement with a potential homicide suspect.

"Were you at the neighborhood meeting last Tuesday?" Todd asked as he followed her along the foyer.

"Wednesday," she said over her shoulder while unlocking the front door.

His shoulders bristled. "Yes, Wednesday."

"Why should I? It was too cold for eating pizza outside." She adjusted her headband.

They probably didn't invite her.

"A waste of time. Every year there's a meeting to discuss the Christmas lights competition, and each year the cul-de-sac declines to participate. Besides, I don't bother with Christmas decorations. It raises your utility bill and clutters the attic."

"I understand."

"Even Abigail stayed home this year."

"Abigail?" Todd asked.

"The cripple."

He winced.

"Mrs. Tipton," Ian said to Todd.

"Roger usually wheels her outside, but even she had enough sense to stay home."

As Todd exited, Ian asked, "Do you sincerely consider Dr. Douglas a suspect?"

Shaking her head, Mrs. Allen said, "She's too smart. This murderer hadn't planned well. They let y'all discover the poison. The doctor is clever. Y'all wouldn't catch her."

"Well, thank you again," Ian said. "You have a lovely home."

Their hostess failed to appreciate Ian's sarcasm.

"Now, it is. The place looked a positive wreck when my husband was alive."

"Sorry for your loss," Todd said. *The man probably died to get away from her—or the cats.*

"I'm better off. When my sister introduced me to my husband, he had been the quietest, most reserved man I had ever met." She shook her head. "As soon as the minister said, 'I do,' the man never shut up."

Mrs. Allen stood on the threshold. "Birds." She snickered. "He would talk all day about birds. At least his binoculars came in handy."

Way to turn a tragedy into a nightmare for her neighbors.

"Surprised he didn't die from psittacosis."

He frowned. "Sit a…"

"Psittacosis. An infection caused by bird droppings." She sighed. "I suppose police officers aren't required to have college degrees."

This time Ian bristled.

"Good evening, ma'am." Todd started to leave.

Following him, Mrs. Allen added, "By the way, why did y'all let the old lady leave?"

He frowned. "Mrs. Lula?"

Mrs. Allen sniffed. "What a silly moniker. Have you noticed how she avoids providing a surname?"

"Perhaps she values her privacy," Todd said, cold and ready to leave.

"I asked her once," Mrs. Allen said, gazing over his shoulder.

A quarter of a minute of silence elapsed.

"And?"

"Told me to mind my business." Mrs. Allen slammed the door.

Good. His appreciation for Mrs. Lula soared.

Todd headed for their vehicle. Thirty minutes with Mrs. Allen had left him exhausted.

"Where are you going?" Ian asked.

"Oh, sorry." Todd shook his head. "That woman—"

"Knows what goes on in this cul-de-sac."

"Such venom."

"Usually, you would appreciate the information." Ian tucked the notepad in his breast pocket. "Perhaps this case is hitting too close to your personal feelings."

Todd jutted in front of Ian, causing the latter to stop precipitously. "Are you accusing me of something?"

Ian laid a hand on Todd's shoulder. "Make sure your emotions aren't clouding good judgment."

With that, he marched up to Mrs. Lowry's front door.

CHAPTER 15

As he left the shelter of Mrs. Lowry's covered entryway, Todd slipped on his gloves and shuddered. "The wind is picking up."

"Where do you think the widow went?"

"Making funeral arrangements or picking up the kids." Todd glanced up at the gray sky. "We'll interview her tomorrow."

Ian zipped up his overcoat. "Want to head back downtown?"

"Not yet." For a minute, Todd surveyed the neighborhood, considering where to head next. He glanced at Myaisha's house while Ian wasn't looking. "Might as well hear from the other party."

"The Stilwells?"

He nodded.

After a half dozen knocks and doorbell rings, the door jolted open.

"Yes?" demanded a tall athletic woman, wearing headphones.

"We have a few questions, Mrs. Stilwell," Ian said, flashing his badge.

A moment later, after fumbling with his gloves, Todd flashed his.

Mrs. Stilwell took a moment to read both badges. "I've already told you everything I know."

"But we have new information which brings more questions."

Her gaze fastened on Ian. "Oh?"

Todd observed her, unsure if Mrs. Stilwell's excitement demonstrated concern or curiosity. *Many people relished murders. Like—*

"Can we come inside?" Ian asked. "It's chilly out here."

"I have a meeting in five minutes," she said, slightly closing the door.

"We'll be quick," Ian said, sporting a smile full of teeth.

Unimpressed, Mrs. Stilwell didn't budge. "What have you discovered?"

Todd observed her shorts and tank top. She clearly hadn't been outside in months.

"May we come inside?" he said, blowing on his hands to encourage entry.

Mrs. Stilwell drew the door closer to her side. "Come back later. I finish work—"

"We wanted to know about your threesome with the Lowrys."

The flush extended from Mrs. Stilwell's gaping mouth to her hairline, giving Todd the response he desired.

"Who told you that? The old crow across the street, right?"

"We can't divulge a witness," Todd said, as Ian removed a notepad from his coat pocket.

Rushing outside, Mrs. Stilwell hustled down the walkway and gave a middle finger salute toward Mrs. Allen's house.

"Get a life, you hateful shrew!" she shouted. A moment later she hurried back inside.

Todd noticed her bare feet. *She must be furious.*

"Well?" he asked, hoping now they would be permitted inside.

"Well, what?" Mrs. Stilwell glanced down at her wet feet. "Dammit."

"Did you have an intimate relationship with the Lowrys?"

"Absolutely not. How outrageous." A snarl convulsed her features. "These ridiculous fantasies. Mrs. Allen wishes someone would invite her to a threesome. Pure fiction. That vicious woman is going to be found guilty of libel one day."

"I believe you mean slander," Todd said.

Oblivious to his comment, Mrs. Stilwell mumbled, "The police ought to look into her husband's death. Now that's a mystery. Fine and healthy one day and drops dead the next—and she received his life insurance. Spends all her money on those cats."

"Mr. Allen died of cancer."

"She hated him. Probably poisoned him and made it look like cancer. No one conducted an autopsy, did they?"

Todd's brow furrowed. "Do you actually believe she murdered her husband?"

"All I know is, one day he talked about buying a parrot, and the next day he died." She smirked. "By the end of the week, she threw out his stuff. That cow didn't waste time mourning."

Ian glared at her.

"Don't believe me?" Mrs. Stilwell pointed her head to the right. "Interview Myaisha. She'll tell you." Looking at Todd, she said, "You two seem cozy. Ask her how Mrs. Allen treated her husband."

Silenced by Mrs. Stilwell's comment, Todd retreated a step.

Ian asked, "Then the late nights at the Lowrys'…"

"We played cards, board games. Family activities after work." Straining her neck to see around Ian, she yelled, "Some of us have jobs. My husband is a lawyer."

Todd followed her gaze. Mrs. Allen stood on her threshold watching. *She has no qualms about spying on her neighbors.*

He needed to be more cautious about visiting Myaisha—at least until he solved this case. Not that they engaged in anything improper, but because he didn't want to give the appearance of partiality during this homicide investigation. Or was there truth to Ian's suggestion?

"How frequently did you and the Lowrys have game night?" Ian said, inching closer to the opened door.

"Who knows?" She shrugged. "I didn't keep count. It was simple neighborly fun."

"But things cooled off recently." Ian made a statement more than a question.

Mrs. Stilwell's thin nose reddened. "Longer than that." Half a minute passed while she appeared to be recalling something.

"Jared lost a major client, started working longer hours—or at least he stayed out later. Our family get togethers decreased, then gradually stopped."

"When?"

Her arms drooped. "Let me see." She glanced upward. "Probably two years ago, maybe less."

As Ian's questions continued, Todd checked his watch. Clearly the comment about a meeting had been a lie. They'd been talking for around twenty minutes.

"Do you have any ideas about Mr. Lowry's death?" he asked as his partner jotted down notes.

A sudden solemnness made Mrs. Stilwell's shoulders stiffen. "No, I don't." She hesitated. "I—I feel bad for Patsy."

Neither Todd nor Ian spoke.

To fill the silence, Mrs. Stilwell said, "She's fragile. I don't know how she'll get along without Jared."

From inside the house, something pinged.

"Sorry, I have to go." Without a goodbye, Mrs. Stilwell shut the door.

On the way back to their vehicle, Ian said, "Who do you believe?"

"There's a little bit of truth in both their stories," Todd said, starting the ignition.

"Back to the station?" Ian asked, warming his hands under the air vent.

"Sure." Todd exited the cul-de-sac. "Oh, wait. I need to stop by an ABC."

"You?" Ian chuckled. "When did you start drinking?"

"I'm not going to drink it, not directly. It's for a fruitcake."

"Your girlfriend is making you a fruitcake." Ian made puckering noises.

Concentrating on the traffic to drown out his partner, Todd muttered, "She's not my girlfriend."

"Then what is she?"

"She's just a friend."

Drumming on the dashboard, Ian sang, "Oh, baby, you got what I need. But you say she's just a friend. But you say she's just a friend."

"You can't sing," Todd said, glancing out the side window.

As they returned to the station, Ian laughed and continued singing Biz Markie, *He's just a friend.*

Despite his comment, Todd wondered if Myaisha considered him as simply a friend. He certainly considered her more than an acquaintance.

She had a boyfriend—a substantially built, muscular boyfriend. However, the fireman didn't concern Todd. It needn't interfere with his relationship with Myaisha.

But how did she consider our association? Should I ask? What if her answer wasn't what I wanted to hear?

Sometimes, he mused, ignorance could be bliss.

CHAPTER 16

As her private office door slowly opened, Myaisha looked up from the computer.

"Hey, lady," Deniece said. "Ready to go?"

Myaisha locked the computer screen and grabbed her purse. "Sure. I can finish charting later."

"Where you want to go for lunch?" Deniece asked, holding the door open.

Waving to her staff, Myaisha departed from the rear door. "I don't know. Nothing interests me."

"Worried about who murdered your neighbor?"

They exited the office from the rear and entered her Honda.

"What? No." Frowning, Myaisha buckled the seatbelt. "I'm worried about my staff. Things have been awkward in the office."

"Because of that pervert?" Deniece asked, choosing among radio stations before stopping on *O Holy Night* by Heather Headley.

"That's one problem." Myaisha paused as she turned left out of the parking lot. "No, I'm worried about how they treat each other."

In answer to Deniece's knitted brow, Myaisha explained how the medical assistants had teased Dina.

"She still struggling with the OCD?"

"It's better, but she can't give up the handwashing and gloves."

"Did you talk to your staff?"

"Briefly." Her shoulders shrank. "I thought I hired people who reflected my values. They were actually mocking Dina."

"Cruel."

"Exactly." Myaisha glanced across the car. "How did I miss that part of their character?"

"People change."

"I don't agree. There must have been a morsel of unkindness inside them I missed when they were hired."

"You're being too harsh on yourself—and them."

"Maybe I'm not such a good judge of character."

Incidents from the past year came to mind—especially regarding the death of her college roommate, Candace. A woman she had lived with for years and loved like a sister whom Myaisha had discovered led a dangerous life, culminating in murder.

Deniece touched her arm. "Hey, I know what will cheer you up. Let's figure out who murdered your neighbor."

"Who cares?" Myaisha tapped her fingers on the steering wheel as they waited at a stoplight.

"You adore solving crimes?"

"No, I don't."

"Um, have you forgotten the last two murders we solved?" Deniece asked, primly.

"I remember almost getting shot—twice."

Dismissively waving a hand, Deniece said, "You focus on the negative." She squirmed in the passenger seat to face Myaisha. "So, who do you consider to be the most likely murderer?"

"D, I seriously don't care."

"What's with you?"

Pulling over to the side of the road, she glared at Deniece. "He tried to get Boomer killed. His bad-ass kids burned my fence. He—"

"Is dead. Three kids lost a father." A moment elapsed before Deniece said, "Patsy became a widow."

Myaisha gave a slight shrug and reentered traffic. "She's probably better off."

"Wow." Deniece guffawed. "Who's the unkind person, now?"

"You don't understand."

"True, Jared could be an ass," Deniece said, holding up a finger. "But Patsy is your friend. The children are the product of their rearing. If Patsy and Jared were indulgent, undisciplined parents, what can you expect?"

"Patsy should have left him a long time ago."

"Judgmental much."

Glaring at her friend, Myaisha said, "I have other things to worry about."

"Is this about you and AJ? Is that why you're in such a bad mood?"

"I have a lot going on."

"Oh, poor baby. Welcome to life."

"Why are you being mean to me?"

"Because you are judging your staff for being cruel and inconsiderate but aren't looking at the woman in the mirror." Deniece gazed out the side window. "Maybe your staff are more like you than you realize."

In the intervening silence, the radio played *Love* by Musiq Soulchild.

"That's out of bounds."

"All I'm saying is, you shouldn't focus solely on problems and forget blessings. Or are you one of those people who only pray about what you want and forget to give thanks for what you have received?"

Myaisha made a scrunched face.

Deniece blew her a kiss. "Tis the season to be thankful, scrooge." Counting on her fingers, she said, "Let's see. You are healthy, employed, financially stable."

"Okay, I get it."

"Have a son who loves you and a sexy-as-hell fireman boyfriend who worships you."

"Does he?"

Deniece gawked. "Why? Did he do something to make you doubt his affection?"

In the restaurant parking lot, Myaisha shut off the engine and laid her head on the steering wheel.

"I don't know."

"Don't know if AJ loves you or how you feel about him?"

Pressing her lips firmly together, Myaisha looked forward as tears clouded her eyes. "I…"

Scooting across the seats, Deniece gave her a side hug. "Hey. Talk to him. AJ will understand."

Myaisha chuckled. "Would he?" If he knew what she was thinking, would he understand. *Would he forgive her?*

Chapter 17

While Myaisha gathered scones into a plastic container, Boomer stretched out along the tiled kitchen floor. His dark, moon-shaped eyes gazed up at her imploringly.

"These are for Patsy and her kids. Move." Myaisha climbed over his elongated body stretched across her feet.

Boomer yawned and meandered into the living room.

Myaisha checked her watch before rushing out the front door. If she hurried, there would be time to prepare before Todd arrived.

Was I excited about seeing him? Watch it girl, playing with fire.

Biting winter cold smacked her in the face. She cradled the plastic container under one arm, adjusting her coat with the other. For the short jaunt to Patsy's house next door, she could brave the cold.

Loud voices reached Myaisha before she walked up the driveway. A seven-foot plastic trellis with wilting foliage partially obscured the front porch. Between the slots, Myaisha viewed Tiffany's profile. The latter's ponytails jostled as she pointed a shaking finger at Patsy.

"Give me those tapes or—"

"Or you'll what? Kill me like you did Jared," Patsy said, lunging forward and glowering in Tiffany's face.

Retreating a step, Tiffany said, "I had nothing to do with that. Jared had plenty of enemies, and not all of them live on this street."

"Liar. Jared wasn't the best husband, but people respected him. He had a good job—"

"For how much longer?"

Patsy gasped. "How dare you?"

"Believe what you want, but Jared got what he deserved."

Audible sobs filled the silence. "How can you say that?"

"Don't pretend you didn't know what Jared did to us."

"I…I don't know what you're talking about."

"That innocent naïve act doesn't work outside the bedroom." Tiffany shifted her weight and leaned forward. "Give me the tapes, or I'll make your life a nightmare."

"You have no leverage over me."

With a chuckle, Tiffany said, "Oh really. Wouldn't the police be interested to know—"

A car horn beeped as a neighbor down the street exited their garage. The two women looked toward the cul-de-sac. Unable to conceal her approach any longer, Myaisha came forward.

"Oh, hi, Tiffany. Patsy."

Tiffany swung around, her face blanched. Patsy tightened the terry cloth robe around her waist.

Myaisha thrust the plastic container forward. "I wanted to drop off treats for you and the kids."

"Oh, hello, Myaisha," Tiffany said. "I wanted to check on Patsy." With a mechanical smile, she swung around and said, "Let me know if you or the kids need anything."

"Uh, sure. Of course. Thank you for stopping by." Patsy crossed the threshold into the house.

As Tiffany squeezed past, Myaisha noticed the flush around her neck, despite the shorts and T-shirt.

"Come in." Patsy stepped aside, allowing Myaisha entrance.

"I can't stay," Myaisha said, regretfully. She truly wanted to know what those tapes contained and the history behind Tiffany's comment about Jared's job. Jared had worked as an accountant for a prestigious firm. *But if he had been in danger of being laid off?*

With the downturn in the economy, she wouldn't be surprised. Prognosticators predicted next year, 2008, would be worse.

Thank goodness medicine will always be in demand.

Accepting the plastic container, Patsy said, "Well, maybe another time."

"Definitely." Myaisha gazed into Patsy's eyes, conveying the weight of the word.

Slightly flinching, Patsy gave a paltry smile and chewed her bottom lip. "Excuse me?"

"I mean, definitely, I will come by and help out." She surveyed the kitchen and front hall. Clothes, toys, and miscellaneous items crowded every corner. Patsy needed a housekeeper—or to teach her children how to clean.

Myaisha laid a hand on Patsy's arm. "Have you made any plans?"

With a sigh, Patsy leaned against the wall. "Not yet."

"Are the kids out of school?"

"This Friday."

"How about an early Christmas gift?"

Patsy's eyes grew larger.

"I employ a cleaning service, for the office. They could come by while the kids are in school and make this place sparkle."

A mist formed in Patsy's eyes. "Seriously? That would be a tremendous help." She glanced around the kitchen. "I'm not the best housekeeper."

"You have other priorities."

"Would you really hire them for me?"

"Absolutely." Myaisha pulled out her cellphone and made a call. Less than five minutes elapsed before she hung up.

"They will try to arrive tomorrow afternoon—I said it had to be before three. Otherwise, they'll come on Wednesday."

"You are truly a blessing." While holding the plastic tub, Patsy gave Myaisha a hug. "Besides you and Mrs. Lula, I don't believe anyone on this street has shown me any kindness."

"What about Tiffany and Carter?"

"Oh, right." Patsy blushed and rushed into the kitchen.

Myaisha followed. "You four were always such good friends." An exaggeration, but she wanted to push Patsy into revealing her true feelings for Tiffany.

"We were." Patsy's shoulders slumped. "Once."

"Time changes relationships."

Staring distantly, Patsy said, "And not positively."

"Hey." Myaisha stepped into her sight line. "I'm here for you."

"Yes." A moment passed before Patsy's gaze focused on her. "Thank you."

A crash sounded from the second floor. Patsy bounded for the front door. "I need to get dinner ready."

Myaisha followed while trying to come up with an excuse to prolong her stay.

"Mom!"

A flurry of footsteps sounded, heading in their direction.

"Things are a bit crazy at the moment."

Taking the hint, Myaisha departed. She turned around to say good night, but Patsy had already shut the door. Glancing into the kitchen window, she noticed Patsy chewing on her bottom lip and the children running around the kitchen opening cabinets.

On her way home, Myaisha considered what she'd learned.

Patsy and Tiffany had a falling out—or had it been between the Lowrys and Stilwells. If the disagreement included Jared, Tiffany and Carter had a motive.

Wait. *Am I becoming interested in this murder?*

Jared might've been a jerk, but Deniece had been correct. Patsy and the kids deserved justice.

She had criticized her staff for mocking Dina, but she had decided Jared deserved to be murdered because he had been a mean, selfish person. The point Deniece had made about not judging others made sense and applied to her as well as others.

Myaisha glanced at her watch. Todd would arrive soon. A perfect opportunity to get information about this murder.

CHAPTER 18

Flipping through the radio stations, Myaisha landed on WFDD. The announcer discussed the upcoming election news.

"Can we listen to something else?" Todd asked, sipping lemonade in her kitchen island.

"Christmas music?" she asked, changing stations. Myaisha stopped on a station playing *Mary Don't You Weep* by Aaron Neville.

"Anything is better than the election or news."

She laughed while returning to the kitchen. "That sounds cynical." Myaisha checked the oven, and with a long wooden skewer tested the cake. "Looks about right."

After removing the Bundt cake, she prepared tea and settled at the kitchen table, nestled inside a nook with a bay window overlooking the backyard. Myaisha watched Boomer sniffing stiff winter grass. In time, Todd joined her.

"Smells delicious."

"I hope you like it." She read the label on the hefty bottle of dark rum. "This is more than I need for one fruit cake."

"Sorry. I couldn't remember how much you requested." He inhaled deeply. "But chocolate cake remains my favorite."

"Mine too." She sipped tea. "The chocolate cake should keep you satisfied until this Friday."

"How long does it take to make the fruitcake?"

"Not long. But the fruit needs to soak at least overnight in the liquor." She rose and removed the chocolate Bundt cake from the oven. "But this is my favorite all time cake." Myaisha placed the Bundt pan on a cooling rack.

Todd sighed and rested against the chair. "Done right, there's nothing better."

As she prepared a glaze to coat the cake, she asked, "Are you ready for the concert?"

"Hope so." He rubbed his forehead. "It's been a while since I played in front of an audience."

"Why?"

"The usual excuses. Busy with work, life." He joined her at the counter and dipped a finger into the glaze.

Myaisha shooed him aside.

"I finally committed and began rehearsing again."

She smiled. "Well, I'm glad you did. What are you performing? Something seasonal?"

"The other performances will be traditional Christmas arrangements." He scratched his head. "I wanted to perform Rachmaninoff, but they requested a piece by Mozart."

Time passed as they discussed his upcoming concert. Once the glaze thickened, Myaisha set it aside.

"You're not applying the glaze?"

"The cake has to cool first."

She prepared water for tea and poured Todd more lemonade. "So, how is the homicide case going?"

He took a long swallow. "Now, why would I discuss this case with you?"

"Apparently, I'm a suspect."

He playfully raised his brows. "Where did you get that idea?"

"From your partner." She leaned across the countertop. "Why didn't you interview me?"

"Because I have been accused of treating you differently than other suspects?"

"Have you?"

Todd grinned but avoided her question. "Is the cake cool enough yet?"

"So."

"What?"

Her head tilted slightly to the left. "Are you going to tell me about the murder investigation?"

"No."

"Seriously? After I baked your favorite cake."

"There's no tit for tat here." He drank the remaining lemonade. "You offered to make this cake before Mr. Lowry's murder."

Myaisha grinned. "Yes, but it would be helpful if you told me what killed him."

"Why should I? You find a way to uncover the details without my help."

"It's the holidays. Call it a gift."

Todd rose and deposited his glass in the sink. "Is the cake ready to frost?"

"It's still warm, but the glaze is thick."

"Can I help?"

"Sure."

Beside her, Todd held a ladle and dripped glaze around the cooling cake. A warm scent of spiced orange arose, tickling her nose.

"I added orange for variety. Fruit and chocolate pair well together."

"Umm. That's tastes delicious already." He handed her the ladle and bowl. "Orange and chocolate sound perfect."

"People are going to suspect you're coming around here simply for my baking," she said, clearing away the dishes.

"It's better than them believing I visit to get assistance on my homicide cases," he said, raising his brows.

They both chuckled lightly. As she cleared away the dishes, Myaisha stole a glance at Todd, wondering about his true motives. He could simply be interested in the desserts. Or perhaps he appreciated her company. Or he could—

Knock, knock.

"Excuse me." Myaisha headed for the door as Boomer raced inside and joined her in the foyer. She viewed AJ from the peephole before opening the door.

"Come in."

AJ kissed her lightly on the lips. "Hello, beautiful." He handed her a bouquet of flowers and preceded her into the living room. His shoulders stiffened as he looked into the kitchen.

"AJ, you remember Todd." She came forward to introduce them.

Grasping Todd's hand firmly, AJ said, "Yeah. The homicide detective, right?"

"Correct."

Myaisha tapped AJ's arm, and the latter released Todd's hand.

"We're making chocolate Bundt cake." She entered the kitchen.

"Sorry, I didn't know you had company." AJ joined her at the island, keeping his eyes trained on Todd.

"No problem." Todd retrieved his coat and gloves from the living room. "The cake's done. I got what I came for."

"It has to cool," Myaisha said, searching for a cake container in the pantry.

AJ sat at the kitchen island while Todd buttoned up his coat.

"I could come by later, when it's ready," Todd said.

"That's not necessary." Myaisha used a fish spatula to remove the cake from the cooling rack and slid it onto the container. "See."

Addressing Todd, she said, "Don't cover it until the cake has completely cooled. It should take another hour."

"Got it."

Minutes passed as she instructed him on how to preserve the cake.

He accepted the container. "It won't last long."

At the front door, he thanked her and departed.

Once she returned to the kitchen, Myaisha started cleaning. Five minutes passed before she asked AJ, "Are you hungry?"

He stood. "Where would you like to eat?"

"I don't want to go out. It's cold and I'm tired."

"Guess baking a cake after work can be tiring."

He held Myaisha's gaze, but she turned away.

"Crazy, but I find it relaxing." She wiped the countertop. "And Todd values my baking."

Rubbing her back, AJ said, "I love it too."

Myaisha blushed and kissed his lips. AJ pulled her gently forward, wrapping his arms around her waist.

"Name it. I'll cook anything you want."

He grinned solicitously. "That's not what I want."

Melting into his arms, Myaisha asked, "And what would you like?"

AJ kissed her deeply then nuzzled her neck. "Come to my place on Christmas day."

With a sigh, Myaisha untangled herself from his embrace.

He frowned. "This again." His gaze followed her around the kitchen, as she put items away in cabinets. "What's the problem? Why don't you want to spend Christmas with my family?"

"Why are you pushing this?"

"Because it matters." He blocked her progress. "My family is important to me. You're important to me."

"I don't want to go."

He held her by the shoulders. "Please tell me why."

Speaking in a rush, Myaisha said, "Because Christmas is special for me and Josiah. I don't want to be with anyone else." Myaisha's chest heaved. Tears teetered on her eyelashes, so she avoided his gaze.

A claustrophobic silence fell over the kitchen. Boomer gazed up at her. She wanted to say more, but the words wouldn't come together.

"I understand." AJ rubbed his forehead. "What about next year—January? We can plan something special, a trip together, only you and I." His hands embraced her waist again.

"Maybe. I don't know." She moved away and returned to cleaning.

"Or we could plan a staycation—visit the Charlotte Hawkins Brown Museum and have dinner."

"Let's talk about it later. It's been a long day."

"Whenever I want to discuss plans, you're tired."

"It's not my fault you started a business while working a full-time job."

"Is that what this is about?" He touched her shoulder, and she turned around to face him. "If you want us to spend more time together—"

"No, it's…" Myaisha paused and took a deep breath. "I'm glad you're doing something to help people find affordable housing."

"What then?"

Myaisha shook her head. "I can't explain it."

AJ headed for the foyer, speaking over his shoulder. "And the detective?"

"What are you asking me?"

His temples tensed. "I guess he simply stopped by for a cake?"

"Yes." She heard a wobble in her voice. *Did AJ notice?*

"Not to discuss murder or for something else."

Her chin trembled. AJ studied her for a moment before departing. He *had* noticed the wobble in her voice.

Seconds later, Myaisha secured the front door before collapsing on the couch. Boomer came to her side, lying his head on her knee. Silently, she cried.

"Mom."

Through tears, she spotted Josiah down the hallway. She hurriedly wiped her face. He side-hugged her on the couch. Myaisha rested her head on his shoulder.

"If it matters, I don't mind going to AJ's house."

She didn't look up at him—couldn't. *How could I explain to Josiah that I used him as a pretense to avoid spending Christmas with AJ's family?*

Secretly, she feared confronting her true emotions. And if she were brave enough to share the truth with AJ, he might end their relationship.

"It's not about you."

He hugged her tighter. "You deserve to be happy. He's important to you, right?"

"AJ?"

Josiah leaned away from her. "Of course, AJ. Who were you thinking about?"

If only he knew…

CHAPTER 19

Winter's gray disposition and rainy weather gave the industrial park a Gotham City vibe. Two multistory duplexes anchored tiny boutique specialty stores. Driving well under the speed limit, Todd surveyed the area, checking building numbers.

"Up ahead," Ian said, pointing at the more austere duplex with a traditional red brick façade.

In under five minutes, Todd found a parking spot. He and Ian trudged along the slick walkway into the building. In the lobby, he removed his gloves while his partner checked the building's directory.

"Second floor," Ian said, shaking water off his rain slicker.

"You take the lead," Todd said, entering the elevator.

"What's wrong with you?"

"Nothing," Todd said, staring forward. He detected Ian's scrutiny.

"Sick?"

"No."

"Shouldn't have eaten an entire chocolate cake."

"I didn't."

"Then why didn't you bring me a piece?"

"I brought half the cake into the office. It's not my fault you missed out." Todd watched the elevator doors opening. "You want me to lead?"

"Don't get huffy. I'll do it."

They walked up to the double glass doors. A gold embossed name plate read Offices of Gilbert & Associates.

As he reached for the door handle, Ian asked, "Worried about the concert?"

Under his breath, Todd said, "A little."

Inside the offices of Gilbert and Associates, an imposing austere receptionist viewed their badges and requested they wait. Todd and Ian sat on upscale-looking—but uncomfortable—chairs under the scornful scrutiny of the receptionist.

"You'd think we came in here wearing speedos the way she's watching us," Ian whispered.

"We certainly do not fit the appearance of this firm's traditional customers," Todd said, sitting bolt upright.

In less than five minutes, an older man wearing an expensively tailored business suit guided them down a wide hall. Photos lined the walls. Plaques attested to the prestige and longevity of the organization.

Once Todd and Ian settled into club chairs before a wide mahogany desk, the man said, "Mr. Gilbert will be with you in a moment."

Thanking him, Todd used the intervening time to view plaques and photos lining the wallpapered walls. One frame centered on a far wall displayed the deceased, Jared Lowry, standing proudly next to other employees in the parking lot below. The date on the photo read five years prior.

"Good morning, detectives." A stout, heavy-set man wearing a pinstriped suit with gold cuff links entered. After the men shook hands, they all sat.

"Thank you for agreeing to meet with us, Mr. Gilbert," Todd said. "We won't take up much of your time."

"No problem." Mr. Gilbert cleared his throat. "This is an unfortunate business. Quite unfortunate."

"Yes," Todd said, wondering how many times Mr. Gilbert would use the word unfortunate.

"Our accounting firm has been a reputable member of the community for nearly one hundred years," he said, gazing at both detectives in turn. "Nothing grotesque like a murder has ever been associated with our firm. This is most unfortunate."

Three.

"It's been most unfortunate for his family too," Ian said.

Todd shot his partner a glare.

Mr. Gilbert blanched. "Oh, quite. Yes, I'm sure."

"Perhaps you could give us some background on Mr. Lowry as an employee. Any problems at work?" Ian's notepad perched on his lap, with a pen poised between his fingers.

"Well…" Mr. Gilbert eyed them as if considering how to proceed.

"Things will go smoother if you simply answer our questions," Ian said.

"The firm would not want anything we share to be brought up in a litigious action by Mrs. Lowry."

Todd and Ian shared a glance.

"I'm sure a firm as prestigious as Gilbert & Associates took appropriate steps regarding any disciplinary actions concerning the deceased," Todd said, his gaze boring into Mr. Gilbert. "However, the public interest in a murder case supersedes any liabilities your company might face."

"Still—"

"If we get a warrant, we will subpoena *all* your records," Ian announced, squaring his shoulders. "Then we'll have access to more than simply Mr. Lowry's performance records."

Mr. Gilbert's eyes jockeyed between the two detectives, apparently searching for safety and finding their stern countenances instead.

Todd leaned forward. "Sir?"

"Yes, well." Removing a handkerchief, Mr. Gilbert dabbed his forehead. "If you had asked me a few years back, I would have said Mr. Lowry had been one of our most promising associates. Yes, quite promising."

Todd nodded encouragingly.

"In the last two years, his performance had declined. A most unfortunate situation."

"Any specific reasons?" Ian asked, jotting notes as he spoke.

"We reached out to Mr. Lowry and inquired. We insisted upon a drug test, which he passed. We recommended counseling—for him and the missus— but he declined. Finally, we paired him with a more senior associate."

"What reasons did he give for this change in performance?"

"The usual. Distractions at home. Problems with the children. All unfortunate circumstances in today's society."

"I take it, things did not improve."

"They had not." His Adam's apple bobbled. "In fact, it had been decided to terminate Mr. Lowry at the beginning of the year. Too unfortunate."

Six.

"You wanted to spare his family the trauma during the holidays."

Mr. Gilbert's countenance brightened. "Correct. We are very conscientious. Family first."

But after Christmas, they would be comfortable lowering the ax.

"Did Mr. Lowry know he would be fired in the new year?" Ian asked.

"We have repeatedly notified—and documented—Mr. Lowry's unsatisfactory performance. His direct supervisor and human resources met with him on multiple occasions to discuss the unfortunate circumstances."

Definitely worried about litigation.

"The firm covered all avenues of remediation."

"Clearly, he had ability," Todd said. "What do you believe made his performance decline?"

With furrowed brows, Mr. Gilbert pursed his lips in thought. A full minute elapsed before he posited, "I believe he became distracted."

Todd's brows rose.

Ian asked, "Any idea as to what caused the distraction?"

"I couldn't tell you." Mr. Gilbert stood, and they did likewise.

"Would you like to speak with his direct supervisor?" As he inquired, Mr. Gilbert pressed an intercom button.

A male voice asked, "Yes, sir?"

Directions were communicated, and Mr. Gilbert led Todd and Ian down a spacious hall with paneled walls into a small conference room on the other side of the building. An enormous metal table occupied the center of the room with tiny surrounding tables. Floor-to-ceiling bookcases lined the walls, filled tightly with leather-bound books and folders. Overhead lights illuminated the spacious room, and the window shades had been lowered.

Before departing, Mr. Gilbert said, "I can presume our cooperation will eliminate the need for a formal subpoena."

Todd shook his hand. "We greatly appreciate your assistance. There doesn't appear to be a need for further communication."

With an oily grin, Mr. Gilbert departed, mumbling about the unfortunate situation.

Rubbing his hand on his coat jacket, Todd said, "You lead."

Before Ian could reply, the conference room door opened.

Extending a warm greeting, a woman wearing a dark double-breasted suit introduced herself and firmly shook both their hands. "Good morning. I am Mrs. Jain. Please be seated."

"Thank you," Ian said, placing his notepad on the table. "We have a couple questions before we let you get back to work."

"Certainly." She sat, ramrod straight with a plastered smile on her face. "We are always happy to assist the authorities."

Volun-told. Todd wondered what Mr. Gilbert had said to convey such a response from an employee.

"What happened to Mr. Lowry's work performance?" Ian asked.

Mrs. Jain placed her folded hands on the table. "Mr. Lowry developed a surly disposition, different than his initial temperate humor."

"Can you explain?" Ian asked.

"Well, he—"

"Mrs. Jain, the more direct you are, the sooner this ends," Todd interjected.

"He had a nasty temper," she said, snapping her lips shut.

The detectives shared a glance.

"Last year Mr. Lowry alienated a major client. I never got the full details, but the client refused to work with him and…" she stirred, "well, we had to make concessions to maintain the account."

Ian smirked. "Meaning you had to give the customer a discount to keep their business."

Shifting in the chair, Mrs. Jain swallowed. "Mr. Lowry had lost several clients in the past two years. We thought he might have a drug or alcohol problem, but he tested negative for both."

"Did *you* speak with him directly about his performance?"

"Oh, yes." Her gaze widened. "Frequently. For years he had been our top performer. Then he…"

As she searched for the proper words, Todd said, "Took a dive."

Mrs. Jain's nose twitched, as if detecting an offensive odor. "Something like that. This didn't happen overnight, but his conduct worsened to where he developed into a completely different person—and a liability. He became incapable of completing the most mundane tasks."

"How so?" Ian asked.

"Angry. Distracted. He complained about his projects being more laborious than the other associates. When management attempted to correct his behavior, he became obstreperous." She sighed. "Such a disappointment. As an accountant, his work had been superior. An astutely capable CPA. Then disaster."

Ten minutes later, Todd drove out of the parking lot.

Scribbling notes, Ian said, "Something must have caused Lowry's drastic change."

"It started outside of work." Todd turned onto the main street.

"In the home."

Todd caught Ian's gaze and nodded. A moment later, he asked, "Lunch?"

"You have to ask?" Ian snapped on his seatbelt.

Checking the time on the dashboard, Todd said, "We can grab something before we speak with Mrs. Lowry. The kids should still be in school by the time we get to her place."

Certain questions shouldn't be discussed in front of children.

"Yeah." Ian unwrapped a candy bar. "I wonder if the widow knows how fortunate she is to have a half million-dollar life insurance policy instead of an unemployed husband."

"Mr. Lowry's murder was fortuitous for his family."

Ian chuckled. "From what his boss said, Lowry wasn't the type of guy to put his family first."

"At least, not to the point of murder."

CHAPTER 20

"What's wrong with eating lunch at home?" Myaisha asked, turning into the cul-de-sac. "I'm trying to cut down on calories."

"Well, I'm not," Deniece huffed.

"Way to be supportive."

"Exercise more."

"I don't like exercising."

"So, you'd rather starve."

Myaisha glared at her friend. As she pulled into the garage, she noticed a recycling truck in front of Patsy's house.

"If I wanted to eat leftovers, I would pack a lunch," Deniece said, exiting the car. "What were you looking at?"

"The recycling truck at Patsy's house."

"She's probably tossing out Jared's crap."

"Figures. It wasn't a happy marriage."

Deniece followed her to the front yard, where they observed three people loading various boxes and bric-a-brac onto a truck. Side by side, for minutes they watched, agog at the number of items discarded.

"Want to check it out?" Deniece grinned.

Myaisha raised an eyebrow suggestively, and they headed over to Patsy's house. They waved to the workers before approaching the entrance.

"Hi," Myaisha said when the front door opened. "We noticed you were discarding a bunch of stuff. Have the cleaners arrived?"

"Not yet." Holding an open box of videos, Patsy allowed them inside. "I thought I'd take advantage of the kids being at school and throw out this junk." In an aside to Myaisha, she said, "It'll be easier to clean the house."

"Smart." Myaisha admired the floors. Because of all the prior clutter, she hadn't appreciated the wide plank hardwood. *Amazing what decluttering did for a room.*

"Need any help?" Deniece asked while walking into the living room.

Patsy darted in front of her and said, "Oh, no. I'm fine. It's been cathartic to get rid of things. I hadn't realized how much Jared and I had collected since the children were born."

"That happens," Myaisha said, surveying the room. "Nice Christmas tree. I like the stockings."

"Thank you." Patsy stood between them and the tree, preventing Myaisha from getting a closer look at the stockings along the fireplace mantel.

"What you got there?" Deniece asked, fingering the videos.

"Just old, animated cartoons. The kids don't watch them anymore." Patsy discreetly retrieved the video Deniece held and dropped it back into the box. "Might as well recycle them."

"You should sell them. People crave original cartoon movies—especially the classics."

"These aren't anything special." Patsy circled around them and handed the box to one of the recycling people. She held the front door open.

"Well, thanks for stopping by. I'll let you know when the cleaners arrive."

Recognizing the not-so-subtle signal for them to leave, Myaisha and Deniece departed.

As she crossed the threshold, Myaisha said, "Call if you change your mind about help packing."

"Thanks again." Patsy closed the door.

Deniece shrugged. "Guess she doesn't need help."

"Those didn't look like children's videos to me. Those covers where blank."

Grinning suggestively, Deniece asked, "Are you thinking what I am?"

Waving frantically, they chased after the departing recycling truck. At the corner, they caught up with the driver. Minutes elapsed as they negotiated a deal for the box of videos. They carried their treasure back to Myaisha's house.

"Mom? Where've you been?" Josiah asked, greeting them in the foyer. "I heard the garage door open minutes ago."

"We were hunting secrets." Myaisha kissed her son's cheek and washed her hands. "What's for lunch?"

"It better be good. I'm starving." Deniece sank onto a stool at the kitchen island.

Josiah prepared two plates of fried rice. "I had a terrific teacher."

"Thank you," Myaisha and Deniece said in unison.

"You taught him how to bake," Deniece said, "and I taught him how to cook." She winked.

"Has estado preparando alguna cosa romantica?" Deniece asked him in Spanish.

"Nada que merece la pena comentar."

"Nadie especial?"

He chuckled. "Nadie, tía D."

"I hate it when you guys do that. You know I don't understand Spanish," Myaisha said, tasting her food.

"Then learn."

Myaisha glowered at her. Deniece blew her a kiss.

"I have a paper to finish. I'll be in my room." Josiah left with Boomer trotting behind him.

Minutes later, Myaisha asked, "Want to watch a video with your meal?"

"Sure." Deniece joined her in front of the television positioned above the fireplace. "Any preference?"

Picking up a video on top of the pile, Myaisha popped it into the VHS.

"Old school. I like it." Deniece curled up on a chair with her plate.

After hitting the play key, Myaisha settled on a floor cushion.

For several minutes, a blank screen scrolled by without any sound. Suddenly, a man's voice could be heard, and a grainy picture of a bedroom came into view.

She pointed. "Look—"

"Shush," Deniece said, leaning forward.

A scantily dressed woman entered the screen. She crawled onto the bed seductively, beckoning to someone off screen by stroking the bed sheets. The video came into focus, and Myaisha recognized Patsy.

She gasped.

Laughing, a woman with long blond hair clad in a negligee, skipped over to the bed. The women kissed before disrobing each other. A moment passed before the second woman's face came into view.

"No way." Deniece dropped her spoon onto the plate. She and Myaisha shared a look.

"Now we know what Tiffany wanted."

"And we found an excellent motive for murder," Myaisha said.

"What are y'all watching?" Josiah asked, rounding the corner of the hallway.

Myaisha jumped off the floor and stopped the video but not before Josiah had seen the screen.

"Y'all watch X-rated videos for lunch, and you worry about me?" He laughed.

"This isn't what it looks like," Myaisha said, removing the video from the VHS machine.

"Don't worry Mom. I don't judge."

"Josiah, please."

"Your mom is too prudish to watch naughty videos." Deniece returned her empty plate to the kitchen.

"Was that Mrs. Lowry?"

"You recognized her face?"

"Yeah." He followed Deniece into the kitchen and removed a soda can from the refrigerator. "Do you think that's what led to Mr. Lowry's death?"

"Not sure," Myaisha said, sipping tea.

He slurped soda before asking, "But you plan to find out. Right, Mom?"

She smiled.

"Ready, Easy Rawlins?" Deniece slipped on her coat.

"Right beside you, Mouse."

"And Mosley's duo sleuths hunt again," Josiah mumbled as he returned to his bedroom.

Before she knocked on the door, Myaisha handed Deniece the VHS tape. A minute elapsed until the front door opened.

"Hey, Myaisha," Tiffany said. "Come in."

"You remember Deniece," she said, softly closing the door.

"Um," Tiffany muttered, studying Deniece. "The nurse?"

"Right." They shook hands.

"So, what can I do for you two?" Tiffany said, guiding them into a sparsely furnished living room.

Though the items were few, Myaisha appreciated their high quality. She rested on a leather couch next to Tiffany while Deniece sat in a rattan swing.

"This is adorable," Deniece said, swinging lightly.

"I know. Can't remember where we found it, but it's one of my favorite pieces."

Cognizant of the time—and her afternoon patients—Myaisha asked, "What did you want from Patsy the other morning?"

Concern and consternation seemed to wrinkle Tiffany's forehead.

She's wondering what I overhead.

Stuttering, Tiffany said, "You must be mistaken. I didn't ask Patsy for anything."

"That's true. You weren't asking," Myaisha said, reclining into the cushions, "more like threatening."

Above her T-shirt's neckline, Tiffany's freckled chest flushed. "I don't know what you're talking about." Rising, she headed for the front door. "Now, if you'll excuse me…"

Myaisha and Deniece followed her.

At the door, Myaisha said, "Then I guess you won't be interested in the videos Patsy threw out."

Though she pivoted as if to exit, Tiffany—as expected —called her back.

"Wait." Her jaw clenching, Tiffany regarded Myaisha and Deniece. A quarter of a minute passed.

She folded her arms across her chest. "How much do you know?"

"We watched the video." Deniece displayed the VHS tape with the unlabeled cover.

Tiffany's complexion paled. Myaisha stepped forward in case she fainted. However, instead, Tiffany leaped at Deniece, grasping for the tape. Blocked by Myaisha's shoulder, Tiffany careened into the wall.

"Ouch!" Tiffany glowered and rubbed her arm.

"Sorry," Myaisha said. "I didn't expect you to rush at us."

"I suppose you told your cop boyfriend about what you heard."

"He's not my—"

"Why don't you tell us about it," Deniece interrupted.

With her head bowed, Tiffany entered a room off the foyer. "Are you going to blackmail me too?"

Given the bookshelves and desks, Myaisha presumed the room functioned as an office. The front window gave a perfect view of Patsy's house.

"I saw the recycling truck, but never thought that moron would throw those videos in the trash." Tiffany crashed onto a leather chair at the desk. "Stupid woman."

Because Deniece sat in the only other chair in the room, Myaisha leaned against a wall beside the window. Speaking gently, she asked, "When did it start?"

"Oh, way back." Tiffany gazed up at the ceiling. "Years ago, when we first moved here."

Mentally, Myaisha considered the year in which the Stilwells and Lowrys moved into the cul-de-sac. She and Sammy had bought their home when Josiah was a toddler. Three families already lived on the street, including Mrs. Allen and the Tiptons.

Did anything strange go on between the Lowrys and Stilwells back then? She couldn't remember. She had been busy with a young son and a burgeoning medical practice.

"When did it end?" Deniece asked, setting the video on her lap.

"Once Patsy became pregnant with their daughter." Tiffany stared out the large picture window. "Jared changed."

"How?"

As Deniece questioned Tiffany, Myaisha viewed photos on the walls and shelves. Tiffany had a degree in computer science and Carter a degree in sociology.

"He became aggressive, demanding."

"So, you called it quits."

A sly grin creased Tiffany's lips. "Didn't bother me— or Carter. I don't mind rough sex."

Deniece's brows raised. Myaisha froze.

Chuckling, Tiffany said, "I know it shocks Myaisha, but what about you?"

"I don't judge," Deniece said. "Everyone has a vice."

"Thank you." Tiffany settled back into the chair.

"Do you know anything about Jared's murder?" Myaisha asked quickly, masking her discomfort.

"No." Tiffany pouted, glaring up at her.

"You have a perfect view of their house." Myaisha pointed out the window. "Did you see anything unusual on Friday?"

"Not a thing."

Both she and Deniece stared at Tiffany.

"Believe what you want, but I didn't. I actually have a lot of work to do." She sighed. "Unlike some neighbors."

"Mrs. Allen?" Myaisha suggested.

"Witch." Tiffany shook her head. "She told the police we were involved with Patsy and Jared."

"Well, she didn't lie."

"It's no one's business but ours."

"Unless it concerns Jared's murder."

Wide-eyed, Tiffany launched up out of the chair. "You can't seriously believe I killed him."

Deniece shrugged. "Why not? You wanted to keep your sexual proclivities secret."

Nice word. I should use it in my book.

"Not enough to murder someone. We've been paying—"

"Blackmail?" Myaisha asked.

Tiffany glared. "And now you want something."

"Only the truth."

"I told you the truth."

Ambling around the room, Tiffany fidgeted with her hands. "About two years ago Jared asked for a loan."

"A loan?" Myaisha asked.

"That's how he phrased it—initially." Running her manicured hands along her hair, Tiffany perched on the edge of the desk. "At first, he kept it friendly. Asked for a few hundred. Told us things weren't going well at work."

"Y'all helped him?" Deniece asked.

"We were neighbors and had been good friends at one time." She looked at Myaisha. "Their boys are barely a year apart, and next came their daughter. Financially, things were tight."

"Jared was an accountant. He couldn't manage his money?" Myaisha asked, regarding Tiffany doubtfully.

"Clearly not. *And* he had expensive tastes." Tiffany sat down again in the leather chair.

Deniece slid to the edge of the seat. "When did the loans morph into blackmail?"

"Carter asked Jared to begin paying back the money." Tiffany took a deep breath. "That's when we discovered he never intended to pay us back."

Myaisha moved closer to the desk. "He made threats."

Tiffany nodded.

"Did Patsy know about it?"

"She denied it, but who knows." Tiffany twisted her thin blond hair between her fingers. "Patsy pretends to be stupid. Opens those large blue Betty Davis eyes and lulls people into believing she's ignorant. It allows her to fade into the background. Typical voyeur posturing."

"It works for her?" Deniece asked, eagerly.

"Absolutely. Patsy took the naïve, innocent act to another level. She excelled at role playing, usually the seductive virgin. Oh, she enjoyed our recreations—until the baby girl arrived."

"So, Jared and Patsy stopped the," Myaisha struggled for a less officious word, 'get-togethers.'"

Tiffany threw back her head and laughed. "For a woman dating two men, you're suddenly Miss Proper."

Frowning, Myaisha said, "I'm not dating two men."

"Humph. Well, you better tell them that."

Stunned into silence, Myaisha wandered over to the door.

Deniece asked, "And the blackmail?"

"Seven hundred a month, for about two years."

Looking out the window at her fence, Myaisha mumbled, "What a jerk."

"He played with fire and lost."

Myaisha and Deniece regarded Tiffany.

The latter hurriedly said, "But I didn't—we didn't—kill him."

"Who do you suspect?" Myaisha asked, perching on the corner of Tiffany's desk.

"Jared didn't pay his mortgage *or* HOA fees."

"Who paid them?"

Tiffany's smile crept up the sides of her face, like a maniacal clown. "The person responsible for collecting the fees."

Myaisha's gaze met hers. The latter nodded.

"Sharon?"

"Yup."

"Why would a sophisticated, professional woman like Sharon be interested in a creep like Jared?"

"Even the devil has redeeming qualities," Deniece said, rising from the chair and pointing at her watch.

"Jared didn't have the voice of an angel," Myaisha said, taking the VHS tape from Deniece.

"Sharon's interest in Jared wasn't connected to his voice." Tiffany blinked sheepishly. "Look further south."

Myaisha grimaced and followed Deniece to the front door.

"So," Tiffany said from behind, "you're going to tell your boy—the cop."

Handing over the VHS tape, Myaisha said, "If it's not connected to the murder, it's no one's business what you and Carter do with other consenting adults."

Tiffany's shoulders drooped as she exhaled. She clutched the tape to her chest. "Carter is considering running for political office. This would end any prospects before he started."

Deniece asked, "Would you be willing to discuss some of your adventures? I'd appreciate details for my book."

"You write too?"

"Romance, not murder mysteries like Myaisha."

"Anytime." Tiffany escorted them to the front door. "Too bad stupid Patsy gave the others to the recycler."

"They're at my house," Myaisha said. "We bought them off the driver. I'll have Josiah bring the box over."

Tiffany flung her arms around Myaisha's neck. "Oh, you're a godsend. Thank you. This means so much to me and Carter. You'll never understand what this could have done to us—if the tapes got out."

"We better go," Myaisha said, remembering she had afternoon patients scheduled.

She and Deniece departed.

On the drive to the medical office, Deniece asked, "Do you believe her?"

"About the ménage à trois, yes. Regarding Sharon…" Myaisha paused while executing a left turn. "Not sure."

"One way to find out."

With a quick glance at Deniece, Myaisha considered how late she would arrive at afternoon clinic if they detoured and visited Sharon. More importantly though, she wondered how many people suspected her of having a relationship with Todd.

Had she been indiscreet? Had there been anything improper in her interactions with Todd?

She appreciated his intellect, and especially their discussions about mysteries and crime. Todd's interest was professional, but hers too—kind of. His expertise added an element of credibility to her stories.

Stop kidding yourself. Their relationship involved more than discussing murder mysteries. But they hadn't been inappropriate or intimate. Simply friends. *Then why did people's comments about Todd bother her?*

To distract her thoughts, she asked, "Are you seriously going to talk to Tiffany about material for your books?"

"Why not?" Deniece fumbled with the radio dial. "I wouldn't use the content for my clean romance books, but it might boost sales of my erotica novels."

"I don't see how you can create erotica *and* wholesome romance stories."

"Two different genres." Deniece found a station and relaxed in the seat as *Step Into Christmas* by Elton John played. "Actually, erotica is harder than people think—to write well, I mean."

"I believe you." Myaisha sighed. "I couldn't do it. But I can't seem to finish a murder mystery either."

"Because you destroy each story before it's completed." Laying a hand on Myaisha's arm, Deniece said, "There's a part of writing which is like a high-wire act. You have to find a balance and don't look down."

CHAPTER 22

Inside the police department, Todd reclined in the computer chair and stretched his legs underneath the desk. With a long sigh, he gazed up at the ceiling. He blocked out the surrounding typing, phone calls, and conversations to focus on what he had just read.

Sitting across from him, Ian glanced up. "What's wrong?"

Though he faced Ian, Todd's gaze drifted beyond his partner.

Snapping his finger, Ian said, "Earth to Todd. You in there?"

"Yes. I'm here." Rubbing his eyes, Todd perused the folder again. "I've been reviewing the Lowrys' finances."

Ian tossed him a soda can. "His boss told us he would lose his job in the new year. I expect their account balances were low."

"But he didn't tell us *how* Mr. Lowry spent his income."

Coming across the desk, Ian glanced over Todd's shoulder, reading the documents. After a minute, Todd handed over the papers.

"Here. I hate people reading over my shoulder."

"You hate anyone getting near you." Ian carried the papers back to his desk and read reports. "How do things work with your girlfriend?" Ian smirked. "Or does she have a special way of touching you?"

Glancing around the room, and lowering his voice, he said, "Watch it. That's how rumors start." Todd drank long and deeply from the soda can. "I told you we're friends."

"Keep saying it and you'll believe it."

Todd sent Ian a heavy glare then returned to typing his notes.

How can I explain my relationship with Myaisha to Ian?

He hadn't even expressed his feelings to her yet—not explicitly—because he believed she understood. Myaisha had a boyfriend, which didn't bother him, but maybe…

He had learned from their discussions about her rather conservative personal habits and beliefs. Having an intelligent, independent thinker to share his ideas with had been refreshing. Myaisha listened well, without criticizing.

They discussed his work, but not simply the gory, morbid aspects. He shared ideas on capital punishment, justice reform, and recidivism. Myaisha contributed her opinions. They debated. Despite their age difference, Todd found her conversation lively and engaging.

But she was involved in an intimate relationship with Thomas. He didn't want any misunderstanding between him and the firefighter—a contest he would certainly lose. Most people couldn't appreciate the type of relationship he wanted. Maybe age gave Myaisha a broader perspective. *She does understand how I feel about her, right?*

"Well?" Ian asked, sliding the papers across their desks.

Todd caught them before they floated to the ground. "Who is Stilwell?"

"The neighbor," Todd said, perusing the papers.

Cutting his eyes, Ian asked, "Which one?"

Once he finished drinking, Todd said, "The one Mrs. Allen accused of having a ménage à trois with the Lowrys."

Ian chuckled. "Oh. The lady who gave Mrs. Allen the finger."

He nodded and saved his report on the computer. "That one. Apparently, she—or the husband—paid the Lowrys a monthly service fee."

"For how long?"

Todd checked his notes. "I searched back one year. Could be longer."

"Wait a minute."

Neither spoke as Todd watched Ian shuffling pages in a notepad.

"There's other money regularly coming into the Lowrys bank account."

"Monthly?" Todd asked, slipping into his coat.

"Using a highlighter, Ian annotated the banking documents. "I found at least five months straight."

Todd frowned. "How did I miss that?" He slipped into gloves. "How much?"

"A thousand."

He whistled. "That's more than the Stilwells paid."

"Wonder what service the Lowrys provided for a thousand dollars a month." Ian's brows raised.

"Blackmail can be a lucrative business."

"Any name attached to the thousand dollars?"

"Nope." Ian rose and hurriedly pulled on his coat. "The finance guys can figure it out."

"Or we can get the DA to issue a warrant." Todd stood. "Let's go."

As the exited the station, Ian asked, "Where first?"

Todd clicked open the car doors. "The widow—if we can speak with her before the kids return home."

"We should've gone out to the cul-de-sac after Gilbert and Associates."

"You're the one who wanted to return to the station."

Ian clicked on his seatbelt. "No intelligent, poorly paid person passes up free food. But we could've made a plate and ate it in the car."

"Easy for you, I'm the one driving."

Todd put the car in gear and drove.

CHAPTER 23

A Santa Claus stood on the corner, ringing a bell beside a red donation box. Myaisha pulled up and rolled down the passenger car window. Deniece handed Santa several bills.

"Merry Christmas," Myaisha said, before driving off.

"You're going the wrong way," Deniece said, shivering and rolling up her window.

"I have afternoon patients." Myaisha turned left onto the street leading toward her office.

"It'll take less than a half hour." Deniece pulled out her phone and placed it on speaker. Myaisha's office staff answered on the second ring.

"Hello. This is—"

"Who is this?" Deniece interrupted.

"My name is Alma. How—"

"Hey, Alma. This is Deniece. I'm with Myaisha."

"Oh, hi."

"How many patients are on Myaisha's schedule for this afternoon?"

"Let's see." Seconds passed. "The two o'clock patient cancelled. We don't have anyone until three thirty."

"Great. She'll be there." Deniece hung up, grinning. "See. We have time. The address is…"

Shaking her head, Myaisha made a U-turn and followed Deniece's directions. Truthfully, she was thrilled to be investigating the murder of Jared Lowry. Though she hadn't cared for him, Patsy and the kids deserved answers—and justice.

This also served as a needed distraction. AJ had called. She realized the time would come when she had to explain to him her feelings. *How exactly?*

Myaisha wasn't sure she understood the real reason she declined his Christmas invitation. She loved AJ, her first and only significant relationship since Sammy died. But she found it difficult to explain her actions.

Lately, she *had* been spending more time with Todd. Though they shared mutual interests and AJ had been busy with his new business, something else lay behind her emotions.

Since their romantic weekend in Charlotte, Myaisha had tried to assert independence, a distance, from AJ. Honoring her Christmas Eve tradition with Josiah provided a viable excuse, but as AJ suggested, they could come by his house on Christmas day.

Why avoid meeting his family? She hadn't met them before, therefore it couldn't be personal.

Dummy. If you ruin this beautiful relationship because you can't deal with your feelings, you'll never forgive yourself.

Ten minutes later, she drove into a parking lot with three tiny parking spaces. Instead of a traditional building, a double-wide trailer had been converted into an office. Laced lattice covered the bottom, partially disguising the trailer posts. In the yard, a sign read Creighton Industries.

Walking up the ramp alongside the building, Myaisha said, "Let me do the talking."

Deniece pouted. "Why you?"

"Because I have more finesse."

"An indirect approach isn't necessarily more refined."

Inside, the trailer had a wide central area. On the left side, a small door led to a square room with a card table and chairs. A narrow door in front of them led to a bathroom. Three other doors led off the center room, and slightly farther into the central area a right hallway extended further into the building.

Seeing no one seated at the square reception desk, Myaisha tapped a silver bell with a sign which read '*For assistance.*'

"Just a moment," a voice from the right hallway said.

An auburn-haired woman, sporting an immaculately tailored sky-blue pants suit, entered. "Yes, how may I… Oh, Myaisha. What brings you here?"

"Hello, Sharon," Myaisha said, accepting the invitation to sit.

"Don't tell me this is about the Christmas decorations. The contest entry has closed."

"No, it's not about that."

Deniece brought a chair from one of the secondary rooms and sat beside Myaisha.

"It's about Jared."

Sharon's shoulders tightened. Unbuttoning her suit jacket, she sat behind the reception desk. "I see."

She glanced at both women while straightening her back. "I'm not sure how this concerns you. From what I understood, you hated Jared."

"Hate is a strong word."

"Am I wrong?" Sharon asked, arching a heavily penciled eyebrow.

Myaisha considered the question before asking, "How long were the two of you involved?"

A tight grin formed along Sharon's glossy pink lips. "Why do you care? Is this about Patsy? Did she send you here?"

"This is about justice."

"Get serious."

When neither she nor Deniece responded, Sharon crossed her legs and stared.

"Oh, wait. I remember hearing something about you being a writer—unpublished of course."

Myaisha frowned.

Leaning forward, Sharon asked, "Is this for a true crime novel? Something your writing group is working on?"

They continued to observe her without responding.

Tapping her finger on the desk, Sharon said, "Surely, you don't suspect me of being involved with Jared's murder."

Deniece shrugged. "Why not? The jilted lover is bound to become a suspect."

"Do the police suspect me?" Sharon's wide green eyes questioned.

"We don't know what the police suspect, but I would like to understand your involvement with Jared."

A blush lit up Sharon's cheeks. "We were in love."

"You knew he was married," Deniece said.

Sharon's hearty laugh shook the fiberglass walls. "Some marriage." Reclining into the chair, Sharon extended her legs and stretched. "Jared stayed with Patsy because of the children. He adored those brats."

Myaisha and Deniece shared a glance.

Suddenly, Sharon bolted upright in the chair. "I hate children."

Deniece gasped. Slightly aware Deniece might be uncomfortable, Myaisha remained silent. Her best friend's ordeal trying to conceive a child remained a tender point.

When the perfect family Deniece and Barry imagined failed to materialize, their marriage crumbled. Years later, after intense counseling, they remarried. However, Myaisha understood the inability to have a child continued to haunt her friend.

Half a minute passed before Sharon sighed deeply. "Jared asked me to marry him, but I refused to live with those kids."

She empathized. Jared's children were hellions.

"He refused to let Patsy have full custody of the kids, so we continued to *live in sin*." Sharon's mocking smile testified to her unrepentance.

"Did Patsy know?" Myaisha asked.

Sharon rose and picked up a photo from a sideboard. She handed it to Myaisha. The photo depicted Sharon and Jared on a beach, their arms wrapped low around each other's waist. Wind blew Sharon's auburn hair away from her face, giving her a buoyant youthful look. Even Jared looked happy.

"She pretended not to. It's hard to tell with Patsy. Jared told me that she faked stupid to avoid arguments." Grinning suggestively, Sharon said, "It worked for their romantic life too. Apparently, she's now using it to get away with murder."

Myaisha's lips parted slightly. Deniece tapped her leg, and Myaisha shut her mouth.

Perched on the desk, Sharon said, "You know about their extramarital affairs, right?"

Handing the photo back, Myaisha nodded. "We've heard."

"Jared and Patsy were swingers for years. They slowed down after they had kids, but Patsy cut it off completely after their daughter's birth."

"Is that when you and Jared started your *association*?" Myaisha carefully avoided the word affair, concerned about offending Sharon, who clearly cared for Jared.

"I can't remember the exact moment it started—the relationship I mean. We started having sex years ago."

Despite trying to remain aloof, Myaisha gawked.

Sharon tittered. "Are you shocked?"

"No, I—" Myaisha blushed.

"There's nothing wrong with good, clean sex," Deniece said.

"Or dirty, kinky sex," Sharon said with a spark in her eyes. Settling back in the chair, Sharon extended her legs on the desk top. "Jared enjoyed kinky sex, BDSM, multiple partners—you name it. He had a voracious appetite."

"And you?" Deniece asked, scooting her chair forward.

"Not all that, but I was up for exploration."

"Patsy?" Myaisha asked, studying Sharon, unsure how much to trust the latter for issues concerning Jared's wife.

"Game for anything—until the kids came."

"When did things become more than play?"

"Once their daughter was born, Patsy ended not only their extramarital relations, but their private, intimate ones too."

Deniece's voice softened. "He felt neglected."

"Lonely." Sharon stared at the picture. "Jared wanted a partner, someone to share his thoughts, discuss his work. He…Jared had an intelligent mind."

Myaisha remembered earlier associations with the deceased. Jared had had a creative mind. When had he lost it?

"What did you suspect when you heard Jared died?" she asked.

"I…" Tears welled in Sharon's eyes. Her feet dropped off the desk. A full minute elapsed while she struggled to speak.

"He drank too much, especially in the last year." Tears trailed down her cheeks, smearing her makeup. "I talked to him about it. He had money problems. It worried him terribly."

"He told you about his money problems?"

Stifling a sob, Sharon said, "Jared told me everything. We had no secrets."

Deniece asked, "You accepted being second?"

Sharon shook her head. "*I* was the most important woman in his life. Jared and Patsy didn't have sex anymore. They barely conversed. If it didn't involve the kids, they had nothing to discuss. He shared his secrets with *me*. Told *me* his desires, his dreams."

"How could you be sure?" Deniece asked.

"Because I understood Jared," Sharon said, eyeing Deniece. "He kept nothing from me, whether it concerned his job, Patsy, or those kids. Who he had sex with and when." Sharon's gaze drifted out the front window. "His dreams. We discussed what we would do when the kids were grown."

Glancing at her watch, Myaisha asked, "Who do you believe killed him?"

"Patsy. One hundred percent."

"She wasn't at the house."

"She could have slipped in the house a half dozen ways. Besides, you don't have to be present to poison someone. As a mystery writer, even you should know that."

Irritated by the insult and tired of Jared's unconventional lifestyle, Myaisha scrutinized Sharon, measuring the veracity of the woman's comments. *Do I truly believe Patsy would commit murder?*

"Motive?"

"Life insurance. Jared worked in accounting. Part of his employment package included a quarter million-dollar life insurance policy. He paid extra out of pocket for the half mil policy."

"You learned about the insurance policy?" Deniece asked, ignoring Myaisha who was pointing at her watch.

"From Jared. We shared *everything*," Sharon said, leaning into Deniece's face.

"If he was having financial difficulties, why did he continue to pay for the extra insurance?

"For those brats." Sharon breathed in and out. "I told you he loved those kids. Besides, he found extra income." The sly cat grin returned.

"Where?"

"I believe you know already."

"Why didn't you help him?" Deniece waved her hand around the room. "You're a successful businesswoman. If you loved him, why didn't you help with his finances?"

Sharon chuckled. "My love did affect my brain. Why would I pay for his family's bills? If Jared married me, I would've taken care of his every need." With emphasis, she repeated, "Every need."

Deniece's brow raised.

"But any money I gave him would've gone toward supporting Patsy and the little rascals."

Jumping up, Sharon eyeballed Myaisha. "Wait. Who told you about me and Jared?"

Myaisha repositioned herself in the chair. "Anonymous."

"Humph." Sharon regarded her nails, presumably while considering how to respond. "The Stilwells."

Perhaps noticing Myaisha's slight inhale, Sharon said, "So, you did know."

Ignoring the comment, she asked, "How could Patsy sneak into the house without being noticed?"

"Jump the back fence. Wear a disguise." Sharon rose. "There are several ways."

"Mrs. Allen or Abigail would have seen her."

"Not necessarily. Mrs. Allen is usually spying out the front window at the neighbors or cleaning up after her stanky cats. And Abigail—"

A phone in the back room rang. Sharon moved toward the door.

"Someone would have seen her." Myaisha rose too, but she wanted to ask more questions before Sharon answered the phone. "Roger, Abigail, Mrs. Lula. There were too many opportunities for the killer to have been seen."

"But she wasn't seen."

The phone stopped ringing.

"What about the poison?"

Sharon frowned. "Have they identified it?"

For the first time, Myaisha realized she had no idea. *How did I forget to ask Todd?*

Because initially she hadn't been interested in investigating Jared's murder. She hadn't cared. Jared had been cruel, and his absence wouldn't be missed.

Not true. His children would miss him. She might not have cared for Jared, but others did. Sharon, his kids, Patsy—maybe.

Did bad people deserve justice? Did justice involve right versus wrong or equality?

The right thing might not equally serve all people. Catching a murderer also meant protecting society, because once someone took due process into their own hands, they would believe themselves entitled to dispense justice at the least inclination. More than a god complex, the murderer would feel entitled to deliver their particular form of law. When would it end?

Distantly, Myaisha said, "I don't know what the poison was."

The phone began ringing again.

"Well, don't fall for Patsy's poor me persona. She's smart *and* manipulative," Sharon said before heading down the hallway toward the ringing phone. "Patsy guessed about…Hello?"

Minutes passed as Myaisha and Deniece waited. As it became obvious Sharon would be on the phone for a while, they departed.

In the car, Deniece asked, "What do you think?"

"I've approached this case wrong." Myaisha sighed and exited the lot. "I need to readjust my position. Start from the beginning."

Because she had believed Jared deserved killing, Myaisha hadn't truly considered his murder from the proper angle. True, he had enemies, but people also loved and appreciated him. Despite how hard she tried to be nice, there were people who didn't like her. One particularly obnoxious patient immediately came to mind.

Didn't her faith admonish her not to judge others? Deniece had chastised her for being overly critical. Myaisha had determined Jared had brought about his own demise and hadn't truly invested in discovering the murderer. Her efforts had been haphazard and insincere. Jared's family deserved answers. And no one had the right to play judge and executioner.

She sat up straighter in the car seat. "We need to get information." As she piloted the car toward her office, she listed items they required.

"Time of death."

"You can ask Todd," Deniece said, fiddling with the car radio.

"Mechanism of death. Type of poison."

"Todd can give you all the details about the murder."

Myaisha sent Deniece a severe glare. "Stop saying that."

"Stop pretending you can't get what you want from him."

Her jaw tensed as she focused on the traffic. "That's not true."

Deniece didn't answer but started singing *Joy to the World* by Aretha Franklin playing on the radio.

Why did everyone suspect her and Todd of being involved? Sure, they had been spending more time together, but it had been innocent—at least from her point of view. Todd simply wanted a friend, as did she. They hadn't discussed their feelings for each other because it was obvious. Though apparently not to her neighbors, friends…

But AJ understood. *Didn't he?* He hadn't questioned her about Todd's presence, except the last time he came by the house, which ended poorly.

She couldn't be intimate with one man and have an emotional connection with another, though apparently certain people could.

Sharon had related how she and Jared had had sex for years before they started their affair. So, for some people, there was a difference between sex and an intimate personal relationship.

How did Todd regard our interactions? Friendly, intimate.

She had presumed they were innocent and friendly, but it might be prudent to ask. What would he say? This might be another time she preferred not to know the truth.

CHAPTER 24

For the few minutes it took to arrive at the Stilwell's home, Todd regarded the quaint neighborhood with its tidy brick homes. Despite the clean, respectable scene, Todd detected an undercurrent of superficiality.

A man had been murdered in his home in this all-American neighborhood. The crime had been planned and executed with malice. Using a disguise or a window of opportunity, the killer had spiked Mr. Lowry's water bottle.

That meant the killer had prior knowledge of the victim's habits—again, confirming his suspicion of a neighbor, friend, or close colleague.

They had interviewed Mr. Lowry's few friends. None had motive or opportunity. Though the water bottle might have been tampered with well in advance of the murder, he doubted the killer would take such a chance. One of the children, or the wife, might have drunk from the water bottle and died instead of the victim. And someone *had* been accidentally killed. He and Ian could find no personal connection between Mr. Lowry and the delivery driver.

Todd drummed his fingers along the steering wheel. The murderer either knew the family wouldn't touch the water bottles, or simply hadn't cared if an innocent person also died.

"I hate winter," he said, turning left and parking next to a mailbox.

Ian placed a notepad into his jacket pocket. "Too cold?"

"And depressing." Todd shut off the engine and exited the car, hurriedly zipping up his coat. "It's only three o'clock but the sky is already gray."

"If your skinny butt exercised, you wouldn't notice the cold as much." Ian marched up the driveway toward the house.

"I exercise."

"Tapping your fingers along a keyboard or strumming a violin," Ian said, knocking on the front door, "isn't exercise. Try running or lifting weights."

"Playing the violin is mental exercise."

Ian chuckled. "That's why the cold air goes straight through your bony frame instead of your thick head."

The front door opened, preventing Todd from replying. He stepped forward.

"Mr. Stilwell," he said, displaying his badge, "I'm Detective Gamble. This is my partner, Detective de Jesus. We would like to speak with you *and* your wife."

"Can it wait?" Mr. Stilwell asked, his bulky, muscular frame blocking the door. "We were in the middle of—"

"No, sir. It cannot."

Ian leaned forward, his badge clipped to his collar. "This is about Mr. Lowry's murder."

Glaring at them, Mr. Stilwell said, "We had nothing to do with his death. My wife and I have answered the police's questions. Now, if you'll excuse me."

Placing his foot between the door frame, Todd said, "We can discuss the money you paid the Lowrys here or downtown."

"Either way, it will be now," Ian added, standing shoulder to shoulder with him.

A flush stood out against Mr. Stilwell's taut neck muscles. "I'm a lawyer and know my rights."

"Good," Todd said with a slight grin. "Then you'll appreciate the nature of a homicide investigation and how motives direct us to killers."

"A man is murdered in his home in broad daylight," Ian said as they tag teamed the conversation.

"The public wants answers and the crime solved, quickly."

"We can exercise discretion, though, and interview you in the privacy of your home."

"Or at the station, where other officers will overhear the reason you paid the Lowrys money monthly for at least the last two years." Todd sized up Mr. Stillwell. "I presume you would prefer privacy."

The air stilled. Mr. Stillwell's icy grimace made the temperature drop further. A minute elapsed. With a deep exhale, Mr. Stilwell stood aside and bade them enter.

"Honey, the police are here."

Wearing shorts and a T-shirt, Mrs. Stilwell entered the foyer.

She must be freezing. Does she have any other clothes?

"What's going on?" Mrs. Stilwell asked her husband, disregarding them.

With a nod forward, her husband said, "They have more questions."

"Oh, of course." Addressing Ian and Todd, she said, "We can talk in the living room."

"No." Mr. Stilwell physically blocked Todd from following her. "We can answer their questions here. It won't take long."

Todd glanced at Ian, signaling him to proceed. If Mr. Stilwell wanted quick, Ian should lead the questioning.

"What did the Lowrys have on you?" his partner asked, removing a notepad from his coat pocket.

"Excuse me?" Mr. Stilwell glowered.

"Blackmail."

Mrs. Stilwell's eyes bloomed. Todd's attention bounced from her to the husband.

"I beg your pardon?" Mr. Stilwell's face reddened. His Adam's apple throttled up and down.

"Stupid doesn't work on you."

"How dare you?"

Though Mr. Stilwell stepped toward Ian, Todd didn't budge. His partner had won multiple weightlifting awards and participated in iron men competitions for entertainment. Ian could easily handle Mr. Stilwell.

"We have bank records," Todd said, directing Mr. Stilwell's ire away from Ian. "Don't bother denying it."

Coming up beside her husband, Mrs. Stilwell laid a hand on his arm. "That wasn't blackmail. The Lowrys were having financial difficulties, and we were happy to help out." She held Ian's gaze. "That's what good neighbors do for each other."

"And it had nothing to do with your relationship with Mr. Lowry, ma'am?" Ian asked.

"You liar," Mr. Stilwell hissed.

This time, Todd intervened, placing himself between Mr. Stilwell and Ian. He understood his partner's tactic, and it had worked, but he didn't want things to physically escalate. The paperwork for such an incident would be prohibitive, even if he would appreciate seeing Ian smack the supercilious attitude out of Mr. Stilwell.

"This is an official investigation and facts are facts." He turned to Mrs. Stilwell. "Are you stating—for the record—that you sent the Lowrys a thousand dollars a month to help with their bills?"

"A thousand dollars, we only paid—"

"Hush," Mr. Stilwell said, drawing his wife to his side.

Todd noticed Ian jotting down the incident. Mrs. Stilwell wasn't as stoic as her husband.

"We have nothing more to say." Mr. Stilwell stomped toward the front door. "If you have any further questions, speak with our attorney."

Ian wrote down the name and number for the Stilwells' legal counsel.

Once in the car, Todd turned up the heat. "Good work."

Snapping on his seatbelt, Ian said, "Easy. He's so wound up, I realized it wouldn't take much to set him off."

"What impression did you develop about the wife?" Todd asked, glancing right at Myaisha's house.

"We should've approached her alone." Ian unwrapped a candy bar. "She's not as reluctant to talk as the husband."

"He's a top-notch lawyer." Before departing, he glanced once more at Myaisha's house, wondering if she had arrived home yet.

"I read he's running for city council—or some other government position."

Todd's mind wandered.

"Hey." Ian smacked his arm. "You listening?"

"Yes," Todd lied, rubbing his shoulder.

"No, you weren't." Ian crunched on the candy. "Fantasizing about your girlfriend?"

Glaring at his partner, he said, "Don't start."

"Why don't we talk to the Allen lady?" Ian shoved the remaining piece of candy bar inside his mouth.

Todd shrugged. "She might have an idea about the money." He made a U-turn. "Might as well try."

He didn't mention it would also give time for Myaisha to return home. He wanted her opinion on the Lowrys. Previously, he'd resisted discussing this case with her. Not only because Ian would have a fit, but he worried about her proximity to the murder.

Todd never suspected she had murdered Mr. Lowry. His principal concern was if the murderer decided to silence Myaisha because she'd discovered the truth. Why couldn't she stay away from his homicide investigations?

However, he had to admit her council had been valuable in the past. It might be again.

He hadn't told her the name of the poison, or any other details about the crime. Todd understood his partner would interview Myaisha, and he'd worried she might accidentally reveal to Ian an indiscretion he had made about the homicide case.

Ian was a skilled interrogator. Fortunately, his partner's interview of Myaisha had been unremarkable. Why did that please him?

Because if Ian understood his true feelings for Myaisha…

Should I trust my partner?

CHAPTER 25

The last dregs of daylight teetered on the horizon, as Todd pulled into the parking lot in front of Creighton Industries. The four-foot sign in the yard practically dwarfed the office.

"Doesn't look like a lot of industry happens around here," Ian said, crumbling a candy wrapper into the cup holder.

Todd scrutinized the exterior. "Is that a double-wide trailer?"

Sliding a notepad into his suit coat pocket Ian shrugged.

"The auspicious name doesn't match the exterior," Todd said, exiting the car and slipping on gloves.

"Aim high." Ian followed him to the entrance.

Todd knocked on the door. Minutes passed. "Doesn't look like anyone's here."

Another minute elapsed before he peeked through the partially closed shades of the front window. He recognized a desk and three chairs. Sparse furnishings, but mostly darkness. From a hallway on the right, he noticed a light.

"Try the number again?"

Ian dialed, but the call went to voicemail. "Do you believe Mrs. Allen?" he asked, dialing again.

Todd's brow wrinkled as he scanned the yard around the office trailer. "She's full of venom but seemed confident."

"Well, if the HOA president waived the Lowrys' annual fees, there had to be a reason."

Stomping his feet to restart the circulation, Todd said, "This isn't getting us anywhere." He pointed. "You go left, I'll check the right side."

"Got it."

Mechanically, Todd checked his gun holster. He inspected the ground as he stepped around the right side of the trailer.

Hedges hid a separate entrance. Parked a yard from the trailer, Todd recorded the license plate of a newer model SUV.

"Whose is that?"

Todd jumped. "Don't sneak up on me."

"Pay attention to your surroundings."

"I can't hear anything over the road traffic." At that moment, a truck barreled down the road kicking up fallen leaves.

Peeking inside the vehicle, Ian said, "Probably belongs to the HOA president."

"If Ms. Creighton is in the office, why didn't she answer the door?" Todd asked rhetorically, not waiting for his partner to reply. Instead, he removed his department issued weapon and approached the side door.

"She is either deliberately ignoring the phone and door or..." Ian raised his brows, not needing to finish the sentence.

With his head, Todd signaled for Ian to stand on the opposite side. Smacking the door with a flat palm, Todd yelled, "Ms. Creighton! It's the police. Ms. Creighton!"

Ian located boulders surrounding the garden bed and assembled a makeshift step stool underneath a window adjacent to the door but higher than eye level. Once completed he said, "Get to it."

"Why me?"

"Because you're the tallest."

Barely repressing a snarl, Todd climbed up on the rocks. He strained to see past the sheer drapes. Surprised, he had to grab onto the vinyl siding to correct his balance.

On the floor behind a cluttered desk lay the body of a woman. Her flaming red hair almost matched the blood splattered across her face.

Cautiously, he slipped down off the pile of boulders. He sighed and shook his head. "What the hell is going on in that neighborhood?"

Responding to his partner's quizzical expression, he said, "Call in the team. We have another dead body."

CHAPTER 26

The front door opened, and Myaisha and Josiah simultaneously said, "Merry Christmas."

"Merry Christmas to you both," Roger said, stepping back to allow them inside.

"We didn't interrupt dinner, did we?" she asked, entering the foyer. Josiah squeezed in beside her as Roger closed the door.

"Oh no," he said, leading them into the living room off the right side of the entrance. "Me and the missus eat early. Better for the digestion." He rubbed his stomach and grinned.

"Abigail," he bellowed. "We have guests."

Myaisha admired an enormous Christmas tree in the far corner of the room decorated with gold and silver ornaments, while Roger grilled Josiah over the latter's university team sports.

She wandered over to the tree, touching the delicate ornaments. "Every year a different arrangement. How do you two do it?"

Abigail wheeled herself into the room. Myaisha walked over and shook hands.

"Hello, Abigail," she said, kneeling beside the wheelchair. "I hope this isn't an inconvenient time."

"Of course not. Please sit." Abigail maneuvered over to the couch.

Myaisha sat in a lounger near the fireplace. "Abigail, did you pick the colors for the tree this year?"

"She picked the colors, but I did the work," Roger said, giving his wife an indulgent wink. "That's how it works around here."

Abigail held out a hand toward him, and Roger took it, brought it to his lips and lightly kissed it.

"Nothing's too good for Abby." He sat on the couch near his wife.

Myaisha noticed a silver band on Abigail's right index finger. "That's new. Is it an early Christmas gift?" she asked, pointing at the ring.

"Oh, no." Abigail turned the ring around on her finger. "This is a gift from an old friend."

"I give her much nicer jewelry than that." Roger's chest puffed out like a boastful school boy.

"Does the design represent waves?" Myaisha asked, inspecting the ring.

"Abigail loves the beach." He leaned over, rubbing her shoulder. "We don't swim and jet ski like we used to, but snuggling up together and watching the waves is nicer."

Lightly tapping his hand, Abigail gave it a playful squeeze. Then she inquired if Myaisha and Josiah wanted something to drink.

Roger stood. "We have cider and hot chocolate."

"They're adults. Myaisha might prefer wine or a cocktail," Abigail said, her forehead wrinkling inquiringly. "Josiah?"

Myaisha declined.

Josiah said, "I don't drink alcohol."

"Not even at college parties?" Abigail said with a suggestive lilt in her tone.

"No, ma'am."

"Every boy becomes a man in time." Roger thumped Josiah on the back and gave him a thumbs up.

"A handsome young man like you probably finds a lot of opportunities to misbehave at school." Abigail studied Josiah, who blushed.

Myaisha regarded her son. What hid behind Abigail's suggestion? What made Josiah blush?

The few seconds of awkward silence gave more weight to Abigail's comment. Myaisha recorded the incident to question Josiah about later. She had believed Josiah told her everything, but lately not so much. Why did Abigail's comment have her wondering about the state of her relationship with her son?

"We come bearing gifts," Myaisha said, holding up a petite box wrapped in red paper with silver bells. "They aren't expensive, but full of love."

Roger accepted a separate, larger gift box from Josiah. "Umm." He inhaled deeply. "Is this the apple bourbon Bundt cake I mentioned?"

"Yes." Myaisha smiled. "I hope you like it."

When he opened the box, a rich aroma of bourbon flooded the room.

"We might get a small taste before bed." His blue eyes twinkled at his wife.

Myaisha glanced at her watch. It read slightly after six. *What time did they go to bed?* Perhaps multiple sclerosis made Abigail fatigue easily. Roger had surrendered much of his independence to care for her.

I should offer to stay with Abigail. Then Roger could have free time to pursue his hobbies. Didn't he used to fly model airplanes?

"The bourbon smells stronger than it is," she said. "I only used a cup in the batter *and* to glaze the cake."

"Bourbon is my favorite," Abigail said, pinching off a corner of the cake edge. "Delicious."

"Not too much, honey. Alcohol doesn't mix well with your medications."

"I promise, Roger, it's not enough to interfere with Abigail's treatment," she said.

"We have to be careful." He patted his wife's hand. "Can't let anything happen to my Abby."

Myaisha noticed a tiny smile on Abigail's face, but the latter's smooth, delicate hand remained stiff. *Was her multiple sclerosis acting up?*

"Abigail, I can arrange for a motorized wheelchair," she said. "That way you don't have to manually wheel that thing around. It must be rough on your hands."

Roger said, "That would be great", at the same time Abigail said, "That's not necessary."

"An automatic chair will protect your hands and allow you to get around easier–maybe get outside more."

"This chair works fine. I don't need to go outside. It's freezing."

"Not now, but maybe come spring. We could—"

"I'm fine." Abigail wheeled slightly away from him. "Josiah, we have a gift for you. It's under the tree. The blue envelope with the green bow."

Josiah retrieved his gift while Myaisha moved to the couch closest to Abigail.

"Here." She handed Abigail the red gift box. "Especially for you."

"Thank you, Myaisha." Abigail opened the box and exclaimed. "Perfume." She spritzed the air, sniffing at the heady scent. "I love it."

While Abigail dabbed perfume on her hands and neck, Roger came over and picked up the wrapping paper discarded around the wheelchair.

"I'll help," Myaisha said.

Because they both bent down at the same time, Roger careened into Myaisha, pushing her up against Abigail's chair.

"Oops," she said, bumping into Abigail's legs.

"Sorry," Roger said, knocking his head against Myaisha's shoulder.

It took a minute for them to disentangle themselves.

"Wow!" Josiah exclaimed. "Tickets to the Panthers' home games."

Still holding wrapping paper, Roger said, "Yep. *All* their home games. And if you don't have a girlfriend, I'll go with you." He snickered.

Josiah laughed, and they continued their prior conversation about college sports.

"I hope you like the scent," Myaisha said, picking at a stray piece of wrapping clinging to Abigail's pants leg.

"Don't worry about that," Abigail said, shaking her leg in an attempt to remove the tape and paper. Because it clung to her pants, Abigail peeled it off and tossed it on a side table.

Moving closer toward Myaisha, she lowered her voice. "I adore perfume, but Roger doesn't buy it for me anymore."

"Men don't consider items like perfume—at least not after they marry you," Myaisha said, conspiratorially.

Abigail sighed. "Relationships change people." Though Abigail addressed Myaisha, her eyes followed Roger and Josiah around the room as they pretended to play football. "Girlfriends get different gifts than wives."

Could she be hinting at Josiah? How come everyone knew about Josiah's personal life but her.

Sammy's unexpected death had brought her and Josiah closer. Their relationship strengthened under their shared loss and grief. Like two people marooned on an island, they held onto each other for survival.

Occasionally, she feared their bond might interfere with Josiah developing significant relationships outside their family. But in time she realized he had adjusted well. With a healthy cadre of friends—in fact, he'd had a short affection for a girl in high school—Josiah had transitioned into college without incident. But as Abigail mentioned, people change.

Had Josiah?

Perhaps over the past few months, she'd spent considerable time worrying about her involvement with AJ and had neglected her son. Distance inhibited more observation of his activities, though Deniece appeared better informed than she did.

They spoke once a week on the phone, but the conversations were stilted. Josiah didn't share intimate details—at least not with her. Did it bother her not knowing about her son's activities or how other people understood him better than she did?

Myaisha had accepted he could speak comfortably with Barry. As a Dutch uncle, Barry represented the male figure Josiah lost when Sammy died. It bothered her, though, how he considered Deniece a better confidant than his mother. She could be judgmental. *Wasn't every parent?*

"…and I pretend Roger and I are dating."

Realizing she hadn't heard a thing Abigail had said for the past few minutes, Myaisha nodded and smiled.

"It's imperative to put effort into your relationships, or they won't last."

The emphasis Abigail placed on the last words made Myaisha flinch. Could her neighbor be referring to her and AJ? How come everyone in the cul-de-sac knew her business?

Fair play, apparently, since she concerned herself with their business. The trials of living in a small city, and on an even smaller street.

Myaisha sighed and rose. "Josiah, we should go."

"Don't worry," Roger said. "Me and the missus don't go to bed for another hour." He gazed down at his wife, who replied with a timid smile.

Josiah gathered up his tickets and followed her into the foyer.

"How's the sleep apnea?" she asked, as Roger escorted them to the front door.

"Better. The CPAP helps a lot." Slyly he leaned his head toward her. "And sleeping in separate bedrooms. Now, Abby can get her rest."

Myaisha gave him a hug and kissed his cheek. "Everyone should have a considerate husband like you."

They departed and headed for home. Roger waved. Half a minute later, Abigail wheeled herself out onto the porch and joined him.

"Go on back inside, hon. It's cold out here. Not good for your MS."

"Good night." Abigail returned inside, and seconds later Roger followed.

On the way home, Josiah said, "Mr. Tipton is a nice man."

"So sweet," she said, hugging Josiah's arm. "He takes very good care of his wife."

"Do you think he ever gets tired of being her caregiver?"

Releasing Josiah's arm, Myaisha regarded her son. "Why? You believe he's unhappy?"

"No," Josiah said, quickly. "It's just…Caring for someone with a chronic illness can be hard. He hardly leaves the house."

A moment passed.

"What if Dad hadn't died in the hospital? What if he'd lived but couldn't walk—or talk?"

Myaisha shifted slightly away from Josiah but made no attempt to stop her tears. "Do you think about how things would've been different if your dad had been unable to walk like Mrs. Abigail?"

Josiah shrugged. "I wonder what things would have been like if he had survived the stroke."

Entering the house, Myaisha choked up. When she found her voice, she said, "I do too."

The low hum of conversation in the police department made Todd's head pound. Leaning over the desk, he squinted at the computer screen.

"Here." Ian tossed a soda bottle across their desks, which Todd caught in his left hand.

"Thanks." He popped four pills in his mouth and chased them down with soda.

"You wouldn't need ibuprofen if you stopped squinting at the computer screen." Ian sat at his desk. "You're gonna give yourself an ulcer."

"My head hurts." Reclining in the office chair, Todd shut his eyes.

"Um hm." Ian tore open a bag of chips. "That's a lousy way to get out of work. If I have to team up with Johnson—"

"I'm not going home. It's not that bad—or wouldn't be if you'd be quiet."

"Worried about the show tomorrow night?"

"It's not a show—"

"Look, don't get pissy." Ian crunched on chips. "I'm trying to be supportive."

"There are three dead people and twice as many suspects. We have no prime suspect other than the widow—who has an alibi for the day of the murder—and Christmas is on Sunday."

Crunching on chips, Ian said, "You worry too much."

"I'm the lead homicide detective. If we don't solve this by Christmas day, the Chief is going to chew my butt off."

Ian wiped his fingers on a napkin. "What difference does it make if we solve it before or after Christmas? The victims will still be dead."

"Their families will have answers."

"Will it improve their holiday?"

Todd glared at his partner a moment before lying his head on the desktop.

Slurping soda, Ian asked, "Are we sure the Creighton murder is related to Lowry's?"

"They have to be related, too much of a coincidence. The nosy neighbor said they were having an affair."

"And you believe her?"

"The Lowrys hadn't paid HOA fees in over two years. Sharon Creighton was president of the HOA. Oh, and don't forget the photo in the office trailer of her standing with Mr. Lowry on the beach." He lowered his head again and closed his eyes.

"We need to question the wife."

"Sure."

Minutes passed as Ian made calls and typed up notes. Todd kept his eyes closed, but his mind remained active. He reviewed details of each homicide. Since he'd arrived at work early that morning, Todd had been considering the cases individually and combined. Piecemeal, he'd developed a suspect for each *individual* murder but not a suspect with a motive and opportunity to kill all three victims.

He stretched his neck and focused again on the computer screen. His vision improved, apparently the medication had kicked in. While his head throbbed less, a solution to the case remained murky. His thoughts jumbled together, refusing to coalesce into a clear picture. *Maybe I am worried about the piano concert.*

"Where do you want to start?" Ian glanced at his watch. "It's one p.m. Our suspects should be in their homes. Mrs. Lowry's kids are out of school, but they probably understand what's going on already. Kids always know more than their parents think they do."

"True, but I hate to interview her with them around."

"We'll tell her to let them play outside."

"It's thirty degrees outside."

"Forty-two."

Todd frowned. "I understand you don't have kids, but that's too cold for children to be outside."

"They won't be naked."

"Maybe we start with someone else." He saved his computer documents and locked the desktop.

"How about the Stilwells?"

"The wife works from home." He wrapped a scarf around his neck. "*She* didn't lawyer up, so we can interview her if Mr. Lowry isn't available."

"Sounds good."

"We'll start with the cul-de-sac then the offices around Ms. Creighton's place." He stood and stretched his arms wide. "Let's grab lunch first."

"Ooh, and donuts for dessert." Ian grabbed his jacket and followed him out of the station.

"You know who we should question first?"

"Who?" Todd exited the police station, pulling up his collar.

"Your girlfriend."

His shoulders slumped. *Not this again.*

Ignoring the taunt, Todd started the engine. As he exited the police parking lot—thinking out loud, he said, "Stilwell lawyered up. I wonder if his demand for counsel applies to his wife. Better check with legal. We don't want anything she tells us tossed out. Mrs. Allen—"

"She likes you."

Todd rolled his eyes. "That woman doesn't like any-one. She is the personification of a cat lady."

"Do you think she had something to do with her husband's death?"

"Leave it for the cold crimes unit. We have our own homicides to solve. But she definitely has the character of a murderer."

"Want to consult your girlfriend?"

Though he detected Ian's scrutiny, Todd continued looking forward and did not respond.

Fifteen minutes later, he parked at their local eatery. Once they placed their orders, he said, "Let's talk through the case."

Ian flipped open his notepad. "Someone poisoned Lowry with SMFA."

"Not in the beer bottle conspicuously placed near his hand."

"You believe the killer did it deliberately?"

"Don't you?" He handed Ian the bag from the cashier then paid for their items. A moment later they exited the establishment in tandem.

"The murderer wanted us to believe Lowry suffered a heart attack or seizure—possibly induced from over-consumption of alcohol. The guy had a drinking problem."

"Then the murderer is familiar with police procedure."

What was his partner suggesting?

Todd sipped his coffee. "There are enough crime shows on television these days where everyone is an expert. Anyone could have tried to mislead us."

"Then the murderer isn't necessarily a mystery writer, or a person who plays make-believe detective."

Feigning ignorance of Ian's reference to Myaisha, Todd focused on the traffic.

Undeterred, Ian said, "Or he could have been drinking beer when the poison took effect. The ME said it would take time to kick in."

"But it isn't soluble in alcohol. The murderer placed the SMFA in water, meaning they had access to the water bottles and knowledge of Mr. Lowry's routine."

"Right." Ian shuffled pages in the notepad. "And the delivery driver's death had been an unfortunate accident. Lowry gave him a bottle of water. The murderer hadn't intended to kill anyone else."

Chewing on a sandwich, Todd said, "Exactly."

"So, the driver got the bottle from Lowry on the day of the murder. When he goes back to the depot, he drinks the water after his shift and dies in the car."

"Makes sense." Todd finished the sandwich before continuing. "But where did the SMFA come from?"

"Creighton's father owns a farm."

He glanced at Ian. "So, she killed Lowry, then shot herself in the head."

"No gun on scene in the office."

"And unless the gun walked itself out of trailer, the murderer carried it away."

"So, Creighton killed Lowry, and someone killed her in revenge?" Ian guzzled his beverage.

Todd's brow rose. "I hadn't considered that."

"It's outside the box, but maybe that's how we have to view this case to solve the murders."

"We agree the delivery driver is out, right? His death had been an accident?"

"I don't know if I would call it an accident. Let's say unintentional." Ian smirked.

Todd gritted his teeth. He turned left into the cul-de-sac, and then drove straight ahead.

Popping up in his seat, Ian said, "You've got to be kidding."

Without glancing at this partner, Todd said, "I'm desperate."

***

"Can I get you another sandwich?" Myaisha asked, extending a tray of cookies, cheese, and crackers.

"No, thank you," Todd said, rubbing his stomach. "I haven't had a BLT in years."

She offered the tray to Ian, who helped himself to two cookies.

"Last call." She again offered them the plate of sandwiches.

"I'm good." He drank his lemonade.

"If you guys don't eat it, Boomer gets the remaining bacon."

The Black Lab scurried off the floor and toward Todd.

"Let him have it," Todd said, eyeing the dog.

Ian grabbed one of the miniature BLT sandwiches. "Thanks."

Myaisha placed the remaining bacon in the dog's food bowl.

"She may be a busybody, but she cooks well," Ian whispered.

Todd agreed and finished his lemonade.

"Didn't expect you to be home this early in the afternoon."

"Josiah's home from college. I wanted to have lunch with him—catch up."

Her eyes appeared glassy, somewhat sad. Was her son ill?

Todd had briefly met the young man, simply to say hello. He had looked healthy, but as a doctor, Myaisha might have noticed something he couldn't appreciate.

She placed the empty tray in the sink and cleared away items. Five minutes elapsed before Myaisha prepared herself a cup of tea and joined them at the kitchen table.

"Did you come to interrogate me again?" she asked Ian.

"We had a couple more questions." Ian flipped open the notepad with one hand while chewing.

"This time it's a double effort?"

Todd ignored the sarcasm. He had wondered how she had reacted to Ian's prior interview but hadn't wanted to discuss it. His partner's insinuations about his association with Myaisha caused enough embarrassment. Todd wanted to be certain there would be no issue of impropriety.

However, their investigation had stalled. He would tolerate Ian's taunts if Myaisha had information pertinent to the homicide case. Besides, Ian didn't really suspect her—at least he didn't believe so.

"We wanted to know if you'd found anything about the murder you'd like to share," Ian said, chomping on another cookie.

"Are you suggesting I've been investigating the murder of my neighbor?" she asked, glancing from him to Ian.

Self-conscious of the playful banter, Todd cleared his throat. "Given your relationship with the deceased and the neighbors along this street, your insight would be appreciated."

Myaisha's grin made him flush. From the corner of his eye, he perceived Ian's gaze.

He sat up straighter. "Let's hear it. I know you found something out."

"Well, I…"

Her pause made him suspicious. *Could she be withholding information?* His hand inched forward to touch hers, but recalling Ian's presence, he maintained his position.

"Are you okay?"

"Yes." She rose and refreshed her tea. "I'm embarrassed to admit this, but at first I was happy Jared had been killed."

Todd noticed Ian's shoulders stiffen.

"But I hadn't considered his family. People loved him." For a moment, she lowered her head. "Jared had been an odious person. He tormented his wife and indulged his kids—regardless of how much chaos they created in the neighborhood."

"You hated him." Ian's blunt statement made Myaisha pivot towards him.

"I tried not to. Jared brought out the worst in me—probably others too." She sighed. "Funny thing is, he used to be quite pleasant."

Todd leaned forward. "When do you believe things changed?"

"Couldn't tell you." She gazed into her teacup. "But I noticed it before Josiah left for college."

"My ears are burning." A voice came from behind them.

Myaisha stood as a lean young man, about Todd's height, entered from the right hallway.

"You've met Todd before." She led her son to the table. "Ian, this is my son, Josiah."

Beaming pride lit up her face. He and Ian exchanged greetings with the college student.

"I thought you were asleep," she said, hurrying to the stovetop. "Sorry, but I gave the rest of the bacon to Boomer."

"It's okay, Mom." He rubbed his face. "I woke up, heard voices, and thought it was Aunt Deniece."

"Sit down. I'll make you a BLT." She rushed to the refrigerator. "Can I get you two anything else?"

Todd declined but Ian requested more coffee.

"Are y'all here about the three murders?" Josiah asked, taking a seat with his back to the rear yard.

Myaisha's gaze widened. "Three murders?"

"The delivery guy," Josiah said, making himself a sandwich of crackers and cheese.

She shut the refrigerator door and stood beside the table. "I didn't hear about that."

"Yeah, Mom. I heard it on the local station. The guy also died from poison, *and* he had made a delivery to the Lowry house the day Mr. Lowry died."

Todd grinned. "Apparently, you inherited your mother's interest in crime."

"Not really," Josiah said, assembling another sandwich. "There's nothing else to do while I'm home."

He gazed up at her. "I'm surprised you and your mystery group haven't been working on it."

"To be honest," Myaisha said, returning to the stove, "I hadn't cared about Jared's death until yesterday."

Ian wiped his mouth with a napkin. "And what did you find out yesterday?"

"Did you tell them about the tapes?" Josiah interjected.

Myaisha shot her son a terse glance.

Todd's brows perked up. What is she hiding?

"I didn't have a chance." She turned away from them and flipped sizzling bacon in the skillet.

If her son hadn't mentioned these tapes, would she have told me about them? Why would she keep it secret?

Ian addressed Josiah. "What tapes? Tell us."

"The Lowrys and Stilwells were swingers."

Ian spat coffee and began choking. Myaisha got him a glass of water while Todd mopped up fluid spilled on the table.

"Sorry," Ian croaked out between coughs.

"Are you sure?" Todd regarded Josiah looking for signs of jest. Simultaneously, he noted Myaisha's solemn face.

"Absolutely. Mom and Aunt D got the videos from a recycling truck. Mrs. Lowry tried to dispose of them."

Todd's brows knitted together over his intense glare. He didn't try to hide his fury. Myaisha refused to look at him, instead tending to the stove top. He'd wait, for now. But she would have to explain withholding information, valuable information, in a double—no, triple— homicide investigation. He inhaled deeply and waited until he regained mastery of his emotions.

"You watched these tapes?" Ian asked, jotting notes.

"I walked in while it was on the tv screen," Josiah answered.

"Then what happened?" Todd asked, still staring at Myaisha's back.

"Don't know." Josiah got up and filled his plate with bacon and eggs. The Lab circled around his legs. "Mom and Aunt D left."

Addressing his mom, Josiah asked, "Did y'all go speak with Mrs. Stilwell?"

"Josiah, you want tea or orange juice?" she asked, avoiding Todd's gaze.

"Orange juice." Josiah sat at the island and ate.

A minute elapsed with no one speaking. Myaisha refilled Ian's coffee and Todd's lemonade. Eventually, she sat at the table but on the side opposite them.

"I know what you're thinking," Myaisha said.

"That you suppressed pertinent information in a homicide investigation," Todd said, tapping his fingers along the table.

"If I had been told another homicide had occurred—"

"You would have shared this valuable information immediately, right?" Ian smirked.

"Where are the tapes?" Todd asked, massaging his temples. The instant they returned to the car, Ian would mention this suppression of evidence. *Why did Myaisha make things difficult?*

"I gave them to Tiffany."

"You what?!" Todd leaped from his seat.

Instantly, the Labrador rushed toward him, baring its teeth and barking. Todd tumbled over the chair to escape the dog. Ian reached for his revolver. Josiah grabbed the Lab by the collar.

"Down, Boomer." Myaisha stepped between Todd and the dog.

His heart racing, Todd kept a chair in front of him. His eyes remained on the animal as he addressed her. "Do you understand what you did? Giving away evidence in a triple homicide investigation."

"It gives the Stilwells a motive for murder," Ian said, holstering his weapon.

Though Josiah led the dog away to a back room, Todd continued standing with an eye on the hallway.

"I'm sorry, it…" Myaisha stumbled to make herself clear. "Those tapes were personal and inflammatory. I thought they should be returned to the owner."

Distraught over Myaisha's actions—and the near assault by the Lab—Todd couldn't speak. His mouth opened and closed repeatedly.

"Technically, the Lowrys owned the tapes," Ian said, "since they filmed them."

"But if they were filmed secretly…"

"Did it appear on the tapes that the Stilwells recognized they were being filmed?" Ian asked.

Myaisha's forehead creased in thought. "It looked like they were aware of the cameras."

"We might not have the evidence, but at least now we understand their motive," Todd said.

"And the reason for the monthly payments." Ian swallowed the rest of his coffee and headed for the foyer.

Blackmail. But the Stilwells paid seven hundred a month. Who paid the thousand dollars? How could they find the answer? And which person finally got tired of paying for the Lowrys' silence?

After giving Myaisha a weighty glare, Todd followed his partner.

"Wait." Josiah rushed into the living room with the Lab on his heels. "Here."

Todd hustled to the other side of the couch.

Ian accepted the tapes while Todd remained at a safe distance. "What's this?"

Josiah grinned slyly. "I kept a few of the tapes."

Myaisha came forward. "How could you?"

"Mom. I wasn't going to watch them." He glanced at Todd. "They were evidence."

Todd nodded appreciatively. Though pleased, he had no intention of moving closer to the young man, with the Lab present. From several feet away, he thanked Josiah.

"We appreciate your help," Ian said before exiting.

Once Josiah and the Lab returned to the back bedroom, Todd headed for the door. On the threshold, he swung around. Myaisha had been following closely, and now they stood nose to nose. "I thought we had an understanding."

"I'm sorry." Myaisha placed a hand on his forearm. "I considered what would be best for Tiffany and Carter."

"Covering up for possible murderers?"

"Protecting innocent people from public humiliation."

He gazed into her light brown eyes and recognized compassion. Wasn't that what he appreciated most about her? An excellent baker with sincere compassion for others—and a clever knack for solving homicides. However, there were limits.

"You should've told me."

"I would have."

"Eventually?"

Her soft smile made his shoulders relax.

"Friday night, after the concert."

"I see." He started to leave.

She called after him. "When were you going to tell me about the triple homicide?"

Without turning around, he said, "Never."

CHAPTER 28

With a rata-tat-tat that would impress the little drummer boy, Todd knocked on Mrs. Lowry's door. He had slipped off his gloves. While they awaited a response, he examined his hands. Would he be able to play at the concert? This case had him on edge.

If he solved the homicides before Friday, he could shift his focus to the concert. He hadn't played professionally in over five years. *Why did I choose this year to break my hiatus?*

Ian circled around the trellis beside the front door and peeked inside the kitchen window.

"Anything?" Todd asked, gloving his hands.

"Nope. No one's home."

"We didn't tell her to stay put."

"Where do you think she went?"

"She might have simply gone to the store. Who knows."

Ian scribbled a on a sheet of note paper and ripped it off the pad. He secured it between the front door and the frame. "If she doesn't call us, we'll have her come to the station."

Todd headed across the street. "Might be better to interview her on our turf, out of her comfort zone."

"You believe she participated in the blackmail or simply played ignorant?"

"She had to be suspicious of the money coming into their bank account."

"Not if he handled their finances."

"True." Todd scratched his head. "Mr. Lowry worked as a CPA. It wouldn't be unreasonable for his wife to expect him to manage their finances."

"Still," Ian hustled in front of him and pounded on the Stilwells' door, "we need to be sure."

Before the door opened, Todd said, "Let's ask forensics to figure out whose name is associated with those thousand-dollar bank deposits."

The door opened and Mrs. Stilwell's face sank.

Did she always wear shorts and T-shirts?

"Good afternoon, Mrs. Stilwell. We'd like—"

"Forget it." Her chin thrust forward. "My husband told you to call our lawyer. We have nothing more to say."

"We have a quick question about videotapes." Ian held one of the tapes up as she started to shut the door. Before it closed, Todd witnessed her mouth drop open.

They crossed the street once more to speak with Mrs. Allen.

The garage door rose as they hiked up the driveway. She scrolled down the passenger window as they approached.

"Can't stop now," she said, hurriedly. "Nimrod swallowed a key."

"Nimrod?" Todd asked, his forehead creasing.

"My cat."

Todd had barely viewed the metal crate on the backseat before Mrs. Allen zipped down the driveway and sped out of the cul-de-sac.

"She's going pretty fast."

"Do you want to give her a ticket?" Ian asked, returning to their vehicle.

"Maybe next time."

They entered their vehicle, and Todd drove off. At the stop sign, he noticed from the rearview mirror, Myaisha exiting her garage. Probably headed back to her office to see patients.

Though he remained angry, his temper had calmed. Myaisha had withheld evidence, but, fortunately, her son had saved it—most of it. If the tapes contained what Myaisha and her son had reported…

"Swingers."

Because Todd had spoken softly, Ian asked, "What?"

"The Lowrys and Stilwells, having a clandestine affair."

Ian picked up a muscle ball from the center console. "I doubt they'd call it an affair."

"How would you suggest we describe it in our report?"

"Married people bumping butts," Ian said, laughing at his own joke.

Todd eyed him quizzically. "Not funny."

"That's because you're a dud."

"Just give me the directions to the trailer office."

CHAPTER 29

For the past ten minutes, Todd had been observing traffic proceeding along the two-lane road outside Sharon Creighton's office. Though not heavy, it moved briskly.

"This place looks different in sunlight."

Ian exited their vehicle and joined him near the trailer. He handed Todd a piece of paper.

"Yep. And it's obvious there are no nearby stores or buildings. This street is well traveled. I doubt if anyone would have noticed activity around the building, with no stoplights or signs to give them a reason to stop outside the office."

"Cameras?" he asked, reviewing the report from the medical examiner's office.

"Creighton has cameras."

Todd's chest lightened.

"But they were turned off."

"Why the hell would anyone have security cameras and leave them off?" He returned the paper.

With a side grin, Ian pocketed the report. "Who said they were security cameras?"

His gaze widened. "No."

"Kidding."

Todd shook his head and walked away.

Ian followed him up to the entrance. "She might've turned the security cameras off to avoid any record of Mr. Lowry's visits."

"In the office?"

"Lowry couldn't invite her to his home, now could he?"

"Why not? His wife wasn't shy on those tapes."

"Well, there were no tapes located here—at least the team didn't find any."

"Where could she have hidden them?" Todd asked, heading inside the office.

"Mrs. Allen could be wrong. Creighton and Lowry might not have been involved."

"But the picture—"

"Of two people on a beach. They weren't kissing or fondling each other."

Todd regarded his partner. "Do you doubt they were involved?"

"Simply playing devil's advocate." Ian unlocked the front door, and they slid underneath the yellow police crime tape. Silently, they searched the office.

"The guys looked yesterday," Ian said, shutting a closet door. "We're not gonna find anything."

"They didn't know about the tapes."

"Are you going to tell the captain about them?" Ian asked, inspecting a rug near the entrance.

Should he? Once he told the captain, the entire department would know. Todd understood why Myaisha returned the tapes to the Stilwells. If their sexual proclivities had nothing to do with the murders, he didn't want to destroy their lives—or careers.

"Don't know. Ms. Creighton wasn't on any of the tapes."

"Not the ones we had. Who knows what the tapes your girlfriend returned to the Stilwells contained."

Dispirited, Todd didn't reply. If Myaisha understood how difficult she'd made their relationship…

Once he wrapped up this case, he'd have to reconsider their situation.

He lifted a drop-down ceiling tile and peered into the space. "We'll tell the captain if it becomes relevant."

He pretended not to see the look Ian gave. A homicide detective had to be objective, but it didn't mean he couldn't be sympathetic. If the Stilwells were innocent of murder, should their private lives become public property?

For a moment, he wished Myaisha's son hadn't saved those videos. Unless the Stilwells were guilty, then—

"Ugh."

"What?" Ian asked, popping back into the lobby from a side room.

"Cobwebs." Todd climbed down from the stepstool, smacking dust and spiderwebs from his coat. "This isn't getting us anywhere."

He sat on the reception desk. "Anything from the canvas of nearby stores?"

Ian pulled up a chair and brought out his notebook. "The closest office is across the street and about fifty yards south. Yesterday, the shop owner mentioned seeing different cars parked nearby. Mail delivery and the gardener."

Todd used a wet wipe to clean his hands, then put on his winter gloves. "Great. Nothing useful."

"He does have a camera, but it's pointed in the opposite direction, and it's grainy."

"We should still check it out."

"On it. I asked two desk guys to view it."

"Later, we'll check it out ourselves."

While Ian scribbled on his notepad, Todd viewed the photos along the walls.

Pointing at a photo, he frowned. "Does Creighton industries own a farm?"

Ian joined him in looking at the black and white photo of a man standing beside a female child wearing pigtails. They posed in front of a barn.

"They manage several HOAs and other properties." Ian peered closer at the picture. "I suppose they could also own a farm."

"Check it out."

"Why?"

"The medical examiner mentioned SMFA is still used by farmers to kill coyotes."

"On it." Ian jotted down a few notes before stuffing the notepad into his suitcoat pocket.

Using a handkerchief, Todd removed the photo from the wall and slipped it into a plastic sleeve Ian held open.

"If Ms. Creighton had access to SMFA—"

"Then she could've killed Lowry."

"But why?" Todd asked, his gaze pleading for an answer.

Instead of answering, Ian replaced the items they had moved during their brief search.

Reviewing the case, Todd spoke audibly but not to his partner. "Creighton might have killed Lowry out of jealousy, but who killed her?" He leaned against the wall and watched Ian tidying up the room. "Mrs. Lowry might have discovered her husband's affair with Ms. Creighton and murdered them both."

"Sounds like the strongest possibility to me," Ian suggested while replacing a potted plant beside the front door.

"But would she risk her kids coming across the poison?"

"She would be nearby to stop them if they found a tainted water bottle."

"But wouldn't her husband become suspicious?"

"There would be ways she could've done it without harming those kids." Ian perched on the edge of the reception desk. "Listen. She has the best motive and opportunity. Hubby was about to be canned. Now, she gets half a mil."

"Where did she get the SMFA?"

"Forensics didn't find any trace of the substance in the house—except for the water bottles in the garage."

Todd stared at the floor. "Which is where he worked out."

A minute passed before Ian asked, "Anything?"

"Nothing."

After one final survey, Todd turned off the lights and they departed.

CHAPTER 30

Outside Greensboro's main library on Church Street, an older gentleman sat on a folding chair strumming a guitar.

Myaisha handed him a twenty-dollar bill. "Merry Christmas."

He removed his hat and thanked her. Admiring his bowler hat, she decided in the future to purchase one like it to add to her collection.

She entered the library and waved to the librarian before heading upstairs. A sign dangled from a chain on the doorknob announcing the Greensboro Women of Color Writers Group *Think It, Ink It* one hour writing session.

At the entrance to the room, Tina greeted her.

"Hey, I heard the police found your HOA president murdered in her office?"

Unloading her laptop and folder from a tote bag, Myaisha said, "I heard."

"The murderer shot her twice." Lowering her voice, Tina whispered, "In the head."

"Brutal."

"Personal." Tina's head tilted toward her. "Did Todd tell you—"

"Gathering details for your next book?" a broad-framed woman asked, glaring at Tina.

"I asked Myaisha what she had heard around the neighborhood." Tina stepped away from the table, but the woman followed.

"Oh, no. Not this time." The woman gesticulated with a long, bejeweled fingernail. "I'm writing this story. You stole Candace's murder from me."

"I didn't steal anything."

"Cerreta," Myaisha said, coming to stand beside the women, "Candace wasn't a story, she was my friend."

"Whatever." Cerreta sized her up and rolled her eyes before facing Tina. "I'm writing a true crime novel about these murders. It's called *The Cul-de-sac Crimes*."

"But they weren't all committed in a cul-de-sac," Deniece said, walking over to the ever-widening circle of women.

"Do you have a title for the story yet?" Cerreta demanded.

Tina sputtered. "No, I…"

"This is ridiculous." Deniece placed a hand on Cerreta's shoulder. "You can't own a story—especially not a true crime. The information is public."

"But I thought of it first," Cerreta huffed, folding her arms over her chest.

"Two people can develop the same idea coincidentally. This isn't a reason to argue."

Cerreta shrugged off Deniece's hand. "How would you react if she stole your story?"

"I didn't steal anyone's story," Tina said, sweat beading on her forehead.

"This isn't the first time someone from this group stole one of my ideas."

"An idea isn't tangible," Myaisha said, as a bell rung.

"There can be more than one true crime novel about the same murder," Deniece said.

"Of course you don't care," Cerreta said, glaring down her nose. "You'll never publish anything. You barely come to any of our programs."

"Actually, Deniece pu—"

Myaisha hushed as Deniece kicked the side of her leg. With a puzzled expression, she regarded her friend.

A shrill bell sounded for the second time.

"Forget this." Cerreta gathered up several books and a writing pad from a nearby table. "I'm leaving."

Tina followed her to the door. "Listen. If it's important to you—"

"Let her go," Deniece said. "Cerreta is always accusing someone of stealing her ideas. I haven't read one story she's finished."

"I haven't finished anything either," Myaisha said in an aside to no one.

"Ladies, please!" Mary stood beside a bulletin board holding a bell. "Time to get started."

Looking directly at Myaisha, she said, "Discussions about murders will have to wait."

"We weren't—" Myaisha began.

"Shush."

Myaisha returned to the table with her tote bag and laptop. However, she had no desire to work on her mystery novel. Instead, she found a clean page in her binder and wrote at the top of the page '*Who murdered Jared?*'

On the next line, she wrote '*Suspects.*' She listed each household inside the cul-de-sac. Evaluating the list, she quickly removed names of people who rarely—from her knowledge—interacted with Jared or Patsy. What did she know, though?

The swingers club had been a mystery to her until this week. *Does anyone truly know their neighbors?* Isolation created peaceful communities.

Mrs. Lula. Capable of murder but no motive. Something was going on with the septuagenarian, though probably unrelated to Jared's murder. *Why did she leave right after Jared died?* No, her exit couldn't be related to his death. But she did depart hastily. A mystery for another time.

Mrs. Allen. Capable of murder but no motive. The cat lady contented herself with spying on neighbors. *Why kill them?* Her life revolved around cats. Local conspiracy theorists believed Mrs. Allen killed her husband. But Mr. Allen had had a weak heart. Despite outward appearances, he had been ailing for years.

Roger and Abigail Tipton. Not capable and no motive. A prosaic couple, kind to all.

In the margin, Myaisha wrote a note to offer Roger a day off from nursing Abigail. Josiah had brought up a significant point. Caring for an ill spouse had its challenges. She liked Roger and Abigail, such an adorable couple.

Many evenings, she, Sammy, Roger, and Abigail had played cards, drank wine, and shared a meal. A year after Sammy died, Abigail received a diagnosis of multiple sclerosis. For a time, she had been bedridden.

Would I have been able to care for Sammy if he had survived his stroke? How would a debilitating illness have affected their marriage?

Determined not to become sidetracked, Myaisha returned to her list.

Stilwells. Capable, especially Tiffany. The strongest motive. Carter intended to run for political office. It might be the twentieth century, but Greensboro residents wouldn't look favorably upon an extramarital relationship—even if the other couple consented. And filming their escapades was scandalous.

The Stilwells had the most to lose. A tarnished reputation would demolish Carter's political ambitions.

Why wouldn't Patsy give Tiffany the videos? Had Patsy participated in the blackmail or had Jared played a lone hand?

Her thoughts drifted to AJ. She needed to cancel their Friday night card game.

AJ would ask why, and she would have to tell him how she planned to spend the evening with Todd. There must be a better way to broach the subject. She would consider it later.

Who else had a motive to kill Jared?

Sharon should be added to the list. She didn't live on their street, but as HOA president, she had spent quite a bit of time around their neighborhood, and her affair with Jared provided a great motive. But as a single woman of independent means, Sharon had options. Would knowledge of her affair with Jared adversely affect her life?

In fact, her family owned properties and businesses all around the Triad. Despite her prostrations of love, Sharon might have been jealous—not of Patsy but the children. Jared refused to surrender custody of the children to his wife, and Sharon *hated* kids. Those kids stood between her happiness and a life with Jared.

What about Sharon's murder?

Patsy could have discovered Jared's affair with Sharon and killed them both. In truth, Patsy had the strongest motive for both murders. Jared had humiliated her, treated her like dirt.

Why had Patsy tolerated it?

She had a good education and had a work history. Perhaps to maintain their family structure; appearances mattered to some people. Though Patsy came off as innocent and naïve, Myaisha recognized a humorous side, too. Playful and engaging with the children and neighbors, but docile and submissive with Jared.

Had that been part of their arrangement? A master-submissive relationship? Myaisha made a note to ask Deniece. She, herself, knew little to nothing about BDSM.

An hour later, Myaisha considered the page and a half she had written. Nothing enlightening sparked from the page. Before she packed up her folder, she scanned her latest mystery manuscript. Garbage. Later, she would discard most of it. The daughter's alibi didn't fit with the scenario she had created. Why did she find it easier to investigate murders than to create them?

Years of writing and she'd yet to complete one story. Useless. She ripped two pages out of her notebook and crumpled them into a ball. Cerreta had been correct—at least about her. She would never finish a story at this rate.

"What's wrong?" Deniece asked, gazing down at her.

"More crap." She started to throw the ball into the trash when Deniece ripped the pages from her hands.

"Let me see."

Women talked and exited the room. Tina made her way to their table.

"What's that?"

"Myaisha isn't happy with her story," Deniece said, handing the papers to Tina.

Grabbing back the sheets, Myaisha shoved them into her bag. "It's a work in progress."

"It takes time," Tina said, looping her arm around Myaisha's.

"Easy for a published author to say." Myaisha walked toward the exit. "You don't understand."

"Different genres." Tina turned off the room light, as they were the last to depart.

Mary shut the door and joined them. "Mystery is oversaturated."

"I'm not trying to find an agent or publish." Myaisha's shoulder sank. "I simply want to finish a story—one complete story."

Deniece wrapped and arm around Myaisha's waist. "You have. Stop ripping them up and throwing them away."

Mary asked, "What was Cerreta complaining about?"

As they took the stairs to the bottom floor, Myaisha said, "She accused Tina of stealing her story idea."

"Again."

"That woman has issues," Deniece said, holding the library exit door open.

"Remember when she accused Lottie of stealing one of her poems," Mary said.

Tina zipped up her coat. "I don't like negative interactions between group members. It's not a good esthetic."

Myaisha patted her on the back. "I'll call her later."

"Thanks."

Tina and Mary had parked along the opposite street. They crossed together and drove off. She and Deniece walked the short distance to the parking garage.

"How do you keep turning out books?" Myaisha asked Deniece. "Maybe I should try romance or erotica."

With her hip, Deniece bumped up against her and pointed ahead at two members of their writing group.

"What?"

Tilting her head and raising her eyebrows, Deniece cautioned her.

Unsure what her friend meant, Myaisha changed topics. "I should stick to investigating murders."

"Speaking of which," Deniece asked, "what's going on with your neighborhood murder?"

She shrugged. "I've not been paying enough attention."

"Is the HOA president's murder related to Jared?"

"Apparently," Myaisha said unenthusiastically. "Then there's the delivery man. Unless he witnessed something and had to be silenced."

"What motive would he have?"

"For which murder?"

"Good question."

They climbed the parking garage stairs in silence.

When they were alone, Myaisha asked, "Why did you shush me a moment ago and in the library?"

Deniece scanned the parking garage and lowered her voice. "Because writing erotica is taboo."

"Where?"

"Everywhere." Slanting her head, Deniece said, "People would think differently about me simply because I write erotica."

"You think so?"

She nodded. "Sex makes people uncomfortable. A person may be held in high esteem, but once it became known they engage in BDSM, society would judge them harshly."

"Humph." Myaisha considered for a moment.

"Homosexuality. Masturbation. These are topics people shy away from."

Their gait slowed.

"Erotica isn't respected as literature. Even romance is considered second class by some publishers. You know how hard it can be to find an agent? Some companies won't even sell erotica on their websites. That's why I write erotica under a different pseudonym than my romance novels."

Myaisha studied her friend. "Are you ashamed of your books?"

"Of course not." Deniece unlocked her car door. "But I wouldn't want my family to find out. You know how they are."

"Yes, I do," Myaisha said, leaning against the car.

"I attend their church on Sundays to keep them happy."

"They should love you no matter your faith."

"They do." Deniece started the car. "I simply want to please them."

"Is there bias in the writing community surrounding erotica?"

"Absolutely. That's why I use different pseudonyms." As she reversed out the parking spot, Deniece said, "Also for anonymity. I can't imagine how my boss or neighbors would react if they read the stuff I write. Not to mention the weirdos out there."

"But it sells," she said.

"Yes, it does." Deniece grinned.

Myaisha jumped in her car and followed Deniece out of the parking garage.

On the way home, she considered the sex tapes. Todd may have custody of them, but Myaisha still wanted to keep Tiffany's and Carter's antics secret—if possible.

Would she be able to? Either way, if the information leaked, she would not be the source. Perhaps she should warn Tiffany—and Patsy.

She switched on the radio and listened to the weather report.

Are all three homicides related? She needed more information. Todd usually supplied details suppressed from the public. Recalling the anger written across his face when he left her house on Wednesday, she decided not to ask him anything until after his concert on Friday night.

"Wait a minute?" Myaisha slammed on the brakes in the middle of the street. The car behind her swerved into the left lane, and the driver gave her the middle finger as they sped by.

Sex is taboo, at least certain sexual activities were. This murder could be about respectability. Tiffany and Carter had the most to lose when it came to personal repercussions. Patsy would too, but people would be more sympathetic since Jared's death left her a widow with three kids.

How did she not know about the sexual trysts occurring between her two closest neighbors? She had been preoccupied recently. Between work and AJ.

Always and Forever by Heatwave swooned from the speakers.

Damn. Should've called him earlier. She had procrastinated all week. *If she associated with Todd innocently, why did she dread discussing Friday night with AJ?*

Darkness surrounded not only the car but her thoughts: a terrible foreboding about AJ's reaction to her cancelling another evening with him.

CHAPTER 31

After refilling Boomer's water bowl, Myaisha scrubbed the kitchen. Once finished, she had nothing else to do but to call AJ. Instead, she rested in a chair facing the fireplace. Mulling over what to say, she finally hit the green button on her cellphone. *Get it over with.*

AJ answered on the first ring.

"Hey, babe. I wanted to call you all day."

"Hi. How was your day?"

"Grueling. I had to clean out a three-bedroom house in High Point. The family left clothes, toys, even food behind. This crazy housing crash is destroying people."

"Sounds horrible."

"Yeah. I hope the family lands on their feet."

"Me too." She curled her legs under her bottom.

"I miss you. Can't wait for tomorrow. I'm bringing—"

"AJ, I have to cancel our game tomorrow."

"What's wrong? You sick? I can come by."

"There's a concert tomorrow night."

"Oh, what a nice surprise. Where're we going?"

"Todd is playing the violin with a quartet. The pianist is world-renowned. It's a tremendous opportunity for him."

"Sounds interesting. Where?"

"It's in Greensboro, but I only have one ticket." Mentally, she could see his face fall.

"I'm not invited."

"They gave him a limited number of tickets." *Probably true.* "And I know how busy you've been recently."

"You didn't want me to come."

"No, I waited too long to discuss it with you—with Todd." How much longer was she going to drag out this lie? "We can do something together another time."

"Like Christmas."

She sighed. "Please don't."

"I'm simply asking."

"And I declined."

Seconds passed.

"So, a whole weekend without seeing each other."

Myaisha's mouth opened, but she had nothing to add.

"Guess I'll see you later then."

"I guess so."

He hung up.

"Dammit." She tossed the phone aside.

Chapter 32

Outside the auditorium, Myaisha meandered toward the exit, allowing the crowd to direct her path. Two twenty-foot Christmas trees flanked the entrance. Silver and gold holiday decorations anchored festive scenes along the walls and ceiling. Angels took flight, blowing trumpets filled with confetti. Gift boxes surrounded the base of each tree. Christmas lived in this Greensboro concert hall.

It would be a while before Todd finished, and she didn't wish to stand outside in the cold waiting for him. Myaisha relished the moment and rested on a bench beside a miniature Christmas tree near the restrooms. She watched the crowd, admiring the glowing faces and festive atmosphere.

From the floor to ceiling windows facing the parking lot, she watched a long line of red parking lights snake along the drive. The concert had been a success. Todd's violin solo received a standing ovation—as did the entire performance. A lovely event perfect for the holiday atmosphere.

A woman rushed in her direction. *Probably anxious to use the restrooms.* Gradually, her face came into focus.

"Myaisha, how are you?"

She rose and hugged Tina. "Hi. I didn't see you in the auditorium."

Wrapping an arm tightly around Myaisha's waist, Tina subtly guided her toward the parking lot. "Ian insisted on sitting by the exit. I'm glad it was music. If it were a play, I wouldn't have seen anything."

"Ma, ready to go?" Ian made a slight head nod to Myaisha, but otherwise didn't acknowledge her presence.

"My legs hurt," Tina said, massaging her thigh. "Would you bring the car around?"

Ian glared. "Ma."

"All those hours on my feet in the hospital." Her bottom lip slightly pouted. "Now be a good son."

Muttering under his breath, Ian strode off.

"Nice guilt trip."

Tina's eyes twinkled. "It's a talent I learned from my parents."

She started toward the parking lot when Tina pulled her back.

"I wanted to talk to you—ask a favor."

Myaisha's left brow arched. "Yes?"

With a deep inhale, Tina said, "I need your help on this murder."

Her lips barely parted when Tina hurriedly said, "Ian won't tell me anything. And he doesn't bring his work home anymore, not since I published my book about Candace's murder. God bless her soul."

"Why are you interested in Jared's murder?" she asked, bewildered by the anxiety in Tina's bright eyes.

"Not him particularly." Tina squeezed Myaisha's forearm. "I signed a two-book contract. The deadline for a synopsis on the second book is due this spring."

"I see."

"Writing the first book had been easy. I knew the people involved and had access to police files because Ian worked the homicide case."

"But this time—"

"He won't tell me anything." A sheen of perspiration coated Tina's forehead. "I guess he received grief from the department about the information included in my first book."

"Why don't you simply write about another murder? There are enough crimes committed to supply you with material for years."

"Yes, but it takes research and time."

And a lot of effort.

"I started on a murder case from about twenty years ago, but it's difficult to get witness statements and first-hand accounts."

"True crime writing isn't easy."

Speaking as if lost in her own thoughts, Tina said, "And it has to capture the public's interest or it won't sell."

"Your first book sold well."

Tina's voice squeaked. "Uh. It did okay."

Her grip on Myaisha's wrist tightened. "But this murder is fresh, relevant. A young man leaves behind a widow with three kids. It pulls at people's heart strings."

Not to mention the salacious sexual angle. Immorality sells well everywhere.

"Sorry about things with Ian, but how can I help?"

Wide eyed, Tina said, "Talk to Todd."

"Me?"

"He likes you. I heard him and Ian talking." Conspiratorially, lowering her voice, Tina said, "Get facts, dates, names. I can't find out anything from my son. He's closed as a clam."

"I'm not sure I can."

"Please, Myaisha." Tina grabbed both her shoulders. "I don't want to breach my contract."

Right then, Ian pulled up to the curb. He rolled down the passenger window. "Y'all done talking?"

Dragging Myaisha along with her, Tina walked up to the car. "No one likes a smarty pants."

"Or a moron," Ian said.

Tittering, Tina slid inside the car. "Isn't he adorable."

"Ma."

The window rolled up as Tina waved and said good night.

For a moment, Myaisha watched their car fade into the chilly night. A strong breeze made her shiver. She considered reentering the auditorium, but instead walked to her car.

Ten minutes elapsed before she spotted Todd exiting the stadium. He searched the parking lot as she drove up to the curb. He hopped inside.

"Thanks." He belted in. "Sorry for the wait."

"No problem." Myaisha directed the car vents toward her legs. "I enjoyed the program." She navigated down the rows before finally turning left onto West Gate City Boulevard.

"Last year had a larger attendance," he said observing the traffic.

"Did you participate in that program?"

"I volunteered with the production but didn't perform."

"Well, you should play more often. It sounded magical."

Todd gave her a side glance. "Thank you, but I played the wrong key during—"

"You're too hard on yourself." Myaisha placed a hand on his shoulder. "They gave you a standing ovation."

He shrugged. "They applauded the whole production."

She smiled. "You played well." She concentrated on merging onto the freeway. A minute later she asked, "Will you perform again—next year?"

"No." He inhaled deeply and relaxed into the seat. "I needed to do this, but…"

"Yes?"

"I wanted to know if my abilities were still at concert level, know if I had lost my skills." His eyes regarded the violin case resting against his leg. "Now I know. Best to make this a one-time gig and end on a high note, while I'm at my zenith."

"It doesn't have to be your last show."

He shook his head. "To play consistently at a professional level requires time and a serious commitment."

"Which you don't have." She gave him a quick glance, but he was staring out the side window.

"At one time I considered playing the professional circuit, joining an orchestra."

"What changed your mind?"

"The pay sucks. The hours of practice are brutal, and…" Again, he gazed out the side window.

Myaisha chanced a look at him, careful of the traffic.

"And I don't appreciate it enough for that level of dedication."

For the next ten miles, they drove in silence.

"You could play for schools and churches, to keep up your skills," Myaisha said, breaking the silence.

He chuckled. "I'd rather play in the park for birds."

"Or street corners for pocket change."

They both laughed.

"Are you going to visit family for Christmas?" she asked, viewing the Christmas decorations on the passing buildings.

"Not while I have an open triple homicide case."

Myaisha scrutinized his face, considering if he carried an accusation in his tone. "I apologize for keeping the videos secret. I wanted to spare Tiffany and Carter the embarrassment. If I believed they were murderers—"

"That's the problem." His jaw clenched.

"What?"

"It's not your position to decide who is or isn't guilty."

Myaisha's shoulders tensed. A heaviness descended between them.

At the stop sign, he glanced at her. "Murder should be left to the professionals. Sure, you have acquired a knack for uncovering clues, but that doesn't mean you should poke around homicides. Murderers are attached to homicides, and a person who has killed three times will certainly kill again."

A beat passed before she said, "I don't simply uncover clues."

"No, you harass murder suspects and interfere with evidence."

Myaisha slightly turned her body toward the door. "I thought you appreciated my help."

With a sly grin, Todd said, "Doesn't mean I don't wish you found a safer hobby."

She turned into her cul-de-sac. "Speaking about hobbies. I prepared a treat to celebrate your performance."

"Fruit cake?" he asked wide-eyed.

"I'm sure there's some left—if Josiah hasn't eaten it all."

His jaw dropped.

"I'm teasing."

Once inside, Todd rested on a kitchen stool as Myaisha sliced a sizable piece of fruit cake.

"Umm." Todd ate while she refilled his lemonade.

"So," he said, wiping his mouth, "anything I should know?"

"Nothing I haven't told you already."

He raised his brows. "Sure."

"From what I've learned, Jared and Patsy were…" She searched for the term.

"Swingers."

"Right."

"What about Ms. Creighton?" Todd asked while chomping on a piece of cake.

Myaisha considered for a moment, staring distantly. "I believe she truly loved Jared."

"Why didn't she give him money to help with his debts?"

"She had no problem giving *him* money but refused to pay his family's debts."

"Some lover."

"Should lovers pay each other's debts?"

Todd slurped the remaining lemonade. "I wouldn't know. Not my expertise."

Did his smile have a special twinkle?

"Sharon said she loved Jared and wanted to marry him but didn't want kids. He refused to leave his kids with Patsy."

"Why? Is his wife a bad mom?"

She thought a moment. "I believe it would be a control issue with Jared. They were his kids, thus he would want custody. Truth be told, neither of them are—were in his case—ideal parents."

"What was the problem?"

"Overindulgent. No discipline."

She sat on a stool next to him. "I blamed the kids for burning my fence, but their parents bought the firecrackers. And their parents failed to supervise them. Those kids do whatever they want."

"While the parents engage in hanky panky."

Myaisha giggled. "Funny."

"And the HOA president?"

"Jared had informed Sharon about his arrangement with Tiffany and Carter."

"And she accepted the situation."

"Sharon wanted Jared but not his kids."

"Oh?"

"Hated them." Noticing his glance, Myaisha said, "Her words, not mine."

Todd rose and stretched. "Well, she had motive to murder him. But who shot her?"

Frowning, Myaisha asked, "Did you consider her a suspect?"

"Everyone is a suspect until they are cleared. She had motive and means. We located some SMFA poison in a shed on her family's farm. Forensics will try to match it to the sample in the water bottle."

"Can they do that?"

"Who knows." He emptied the glass of lemonade.

"Did you consider me a suspect?" she asked, following him to the front door.

"Absolutely." He slipped on his coat and gloves. "I thought if anyone had the intelligence to commit this crime and get away with it, you did."

"Nice. Glad I know how you feel about me." She grabbed a coat and opened the front door. "And the delivery driver?"

"Innocent bystander."

"Or he could have been a witness. Maybe he saw something, and the murderer silenced him before he could contact the police."

"Far-fetched."

"Possible."

"In a novel."

Her head tilted to the side.

"Okay. If we go with your scenario, why didn't the delivery driver contact the police?"

Furrows multiplied across her forehead as she thought. "He didn't have time. Didn't understand the importance of what he witnessed. Or he blackmailed the killer."

Todd held up his hands in surrender. "Please. Not tonight. Sorry I asked."

Before she stepped outside, Todd gave her a peck on the cheek. "You're a delightful person. Thank you for tonight."

He departed.

Myaisha followed him down the cement walkway. As Todd headed for his car, she noticed a large double-wide truck at the foot of her driveway.

In the front seat, AJ watched, his hands clutching the steering wheel.

How long has he been parked there?

Todd raised his brow in a greeting toward AJ, then got in his car and drove off. However, AJ remained inside his truck.

Should she approach him? He could get out of the truck if he wanted to talk.

They stared at each other but neither moved. A minute passed, then another before AJ drove off. She watched his taillights disappear into the night.

Myaisha returned inside, determined not to call him.

She hadn't expected Todd to kiss her. It had been innocent. They were friends. Or had she misjudged Todd's affection?

CHAPTER 33

The police station had emptied hours ago. Todd refilled his coffee and returned to his desk. In the detectives' department, a two-foot Christmas tree with a half dozen ornaments and a tinsel star shimmered in the corner with its alternating multicolored lights.

"How long are you hanging around the station?" Ian said, buttoning up his overcoat.

Todd sipped lukewarm coffee. "Probably another hour. There's no reason to rush out of here since I'm not driving down to my parents' house."

"You're welcome to spend Christmas Eve with us."

"What's your mom cooking?" Todd asked, glancing up from the computer screen.

"All my favorites," Ian said with a wide, toothy grin.

"Thanks, but I'm good." He leaned back in the chair. "Bring in any leftovers."

Chuckling, Ian said, "Dude, there won't be any."

"Here." Todd slid two wrapped gifts across their desks. "Merry Christmas."

Ian picked up the packages and read the stickers. "One for my mom?"

"Yes. She's a sweet woman."

"You're a pushover for a woman who cooks."

"Who cooks *well*." Todd grinned. "Wish her a Merry Christmas from me."

Shaking the other smaller, thinner box, Ian asked, "What did you get me?"

"Open it and find out."

"Naw. I'll wait until tomorrow." He tucked the boxes under his arm. "Sorry I didn't get you anything."

"Bring me leftovers."

Ian walked around the desk and glanced over Todd's shoulder. "What are you working on?"

"Going over witness statements."

"Anything significant?"

Todd rubbed his forehead. "I'm not sure, but…"

"What?"

"Mrs. Lula and Mrs. Allen both mentioned a gardener in the neighborhood on Friday before Mr. Lowry's murder."

"So?"

"No one who lives in the cul-de-sac employs a gardener."

"You sure?"

Todd clicked through pages of his online report. "They all denied it."

"They could be lying."

"Why?"

Ian shrugged.

"Remember the witness statements on the Creighton murder?" he asked.

"There wasn't a gardener involved."

"The guy up the street mentioned a gardener roaming around the back of Creighton's office near the hedges."

"Don't tell me."

Todd nodded. "The office receptionist stated their landscaper comes twice a month and wasn't scheduled to work on the day of the murder."

Ian set the boxes on the table as he read Todd's notes. "It could be important."

"A murderer disguised as a gardener would be original."

"When have you ever paid attention to a landscaper?" Ian rested on the corner of Todd's desk. "Great camouflage."

"True."

For a full minute, neither spoke.

"Well?" Ian asked, sliding off the desk and picking up the packages.

"Something to look into." He considered the cold mug of coffee, then pushed it aside. "It can wait until Monday."

Todd stood. "Have a Merry Christmas."

They exchanged a bro hug.

"Take care man." Ian began to depart. "If you change your mind and get hungry, drop by."

"Will do."

Over the next hour, Todd reread all the case notes. "Screw this." He made a call.

Hope she doesn't mind.

The call went to voicemail. *What message should I leave?*

He stared at the cellphone for a half minute, then dropped it into his coat pocket.

"Never mind."

As he exited the station, his cellphone rang.

Chapter 34

Christmas lights twinkled, casting a shadow against the far wall of the living room. Myaisha curled up on the couch, admiring the tree. Boomer lounged on the floor at her feet. His snoring amplified around the otherwise silent house.

The abbreviated church service had allowed her to return home before lunch. She and Josiah had a late breakfast. Now, he snoozed in his room. The perfect ending to a lovely Christmas day.

She skimmed the latest book on her to-be-read list. Actually, she had managed to whittle the list down to under twenty books—the shortest it had ever been since she started keeping a list.

Myaisha inhaled the holiday-scented tea, carefully sipping the piping hot liquid. If she could bottle this moment of peace…

Gradually, she drifted off to sleep.

Ding dong. Ding dong.

The doorbell startled her awake. Boomer raced down the foyer, barking and circling the front door, growling, with the fur on his back raised.

From the peephole, Myaisha saw Todd shivering and holding a gift box.

"Merry Christmas!" She invited him inside.

Todd's gaze zeroed in on the Lab.

"Boomer, move."

The Lab sniffed around Todd's feet before retreating to the living room.

He handed her the red and gold box. "Merry Christmas."

"Thank you." She led him into the kitchen. "And I have something you'll appreciate."

Leaving the box on a table in the living room, Myaisha poured Todd lemonade and sliced him a huge piece of chocolate caramel cake.

"It's Josiah's favorite." She licked frosting off her fingers. "I make it for his birthday and holidays."

After taking a large bite, Todd's eyes closed. "Umm." He ate half the slice of cake. "It's my new favorite."

"Thank you." She joined him at the island. "Is this a purely social visit?"

"It is now."

"You didn't want to drive home for at least one day?"

"Most of my family live around DC. That's too far for one day."

"Interstate 95 is a nightmare."

"And worse during the holidays."

The tea kettle whistled. As she prepared tea, Myaisha asked, "Why did you move away from your family?"

"They moved to DC when my sister received orders to a base in Virginia."

Recalling how Todd's sister died, Myaisha allowed a moment to pass, then rejoined him at the island with a steaming cup of tea.

"Well, you should visit."

Todd wiped his mouth. "I do. Christmas isn't as important a holiday for me as New Year's."

Myaisha sliced another piece of cake for Todd. "So, what did you want to ask me?"

"This isn't an interrogation."

"Good to know." She sliced a much smaller piece of cake for herself. "Besides, your partner already conducted the official interview at my office."

Todd avoided her gaze and devoured the cake.

"Was it your idea or his?"

"It wasn't an option."

He drank lemonade while looking at the Christmas tree. "Do you and Josiah exchange gifts?"

"We have a one gift minimum." Under the tree, Myaisha removed a small thin envelope. "This is for you."

Todd's brows rose.

"I forgot to give it to you on Friday night."

"Thank you." He tore open the envelope. "A season pass to the Charlotte orchestra."

Myaisha observed his expression. "There are two passes. Easier to take a friend, if you want."

"That's very considerate. Thank you."

They glanced at each other, then Myaisha sat on the couch facing the backyard. "Anyway, I thought it fit you."

"It's perfect."

Another moment passed. *Does he not like it? Maybe I shouldn't have given him two tickets. Does he believe I meant for him to ask me to accompany him?*

"Well, I had a couple questions—about the murder." Todd carried his glass of lemonade to the living room and sat on the couch facing the fireplace and Christmas tree. "Hope you don't mind," he asked Myaisha, who sat on a couch to his left.

"I understand. Patsy and the kids deserve answers."

"Yesterday, I reviewed my case notes. Two of your neighbors mentioned seeing a gardener the day Lowry died."

Myaisha's brow furrowed. "Gardener."

"Yes. But no one admitted to hiring one."

"No one in this cul-de-sac hires a professional gardener." Her forehead creased in thought. "Are you sure they didn't mean they watched someone gardening?"

Todd shook his head. "They noticed a gardener around this end of the street."

"Who said that?"

He hesitated.

"Is it privileged information?"

"I…" He studied her while finishing his lemonade. "This stays between us."

"Of course."

He smirked as his eyebrows rose. "Not even your writing club."

Myaisha took a deep breath. "Fine."

"Mrs. Lula and Mrs. Allen."

She considered the two women. Both were known for being observant. Of the two, she placed more reliance on Mrs. Lula.

"There's no reason to doubt what they reported, but it makes no sense. I can't remember anyone in the cul-de-sac employing a gardener or landscaper." Myaisha circled the living room as she thought over the information. "The only thing I can come up with—"

"Is the murderer disguised themselves as a gardener," Todd interrupted.

"Clever."

"And effective." He retrieved more lemonade from the pitcher on the kitchen island. "I wanted to question Mrs. Lula again but she's not been home."

"She left town," Myaisha said distantly. Her mind weighed the possibility of an outsider masquerading as a gardener. Had she noticed anyone unusual on Friday?

Her mind had focused on the fence and Boomer—and her conversation with the lawyer about protecting her home and Labrador.

"Do you believe the murderer is a resident of this cul-de-sac?" Myaisha asked.

"We did until Ms. Creighton's murder."

Myaisha shivered, palming her tea to warm her hands. "Why Sharon?"

"Did you know her well?"

"No, but we spoke with her that afternoon."

Todd's back stiffened. "And you didn't tell me."

"There wasn't time." She spoke rapidly. "By the time I heard about her death, we…you were upset with me about the sex tapes. Then I had the fruit cake to prepare before the concert, and I didn't want to discuss murder before your performance. After, well, I was excited about the concert."

His terse gaze made her fidget.

"It didn't seem significant. I mean, we were going to talk soon, and I planned to tell you then."

He drummed his fingers along the couch cushion. "Her dad owns a farm."

"I discovered they owned multiple properties."

"Farmers use SMFA to kill coyotes."

He was leading her somewhere. *Why?*

Her gaze widened. "You suspect Sharon killed Jared?"

"Why not?"

"She loved him."

"You know this because…"

"She admitted it."

"And you believed her."

Myaisha sat down again. "Yes. If you'd been there, you would too."

"I would've been happy to join you ladies, if someone had notified me of the impromptu meeting."

She ignored his sarcasm.

"Ms. Creighton was successful. Mr. Lowry had a desperate need for money. She wanted to marry him but didn't mind watching him go broke?"

"She didn't give money to men, not her style."

"Wow."

"Even if he'd declared bankruptcy, he wouldn't have been on the streets. She would've bailed him out."

"But let his kids and wife be homeless."

She shrugged. "People are complicated."

"But she let him skate on the HOA fees?"

Myaisha leaned back against the pillows and gazed up at the ceiling. "Jared definitely couldn't afford a gardener."

Resting his elbows on his knees, Todd said, "A witness noticed a gardener around Creighton's office the day she died."

Myaisha's brow arched. "Interesting."

Todd nodded.

"So, you believe one person murdered them both."

"Possibly. The wife has the best motive. I'm not sure how she got hold of the SMFA, but she greatly benefits from his death." Todd gave a brief synopsis of what he'd learned from Jared's employer. Afterward, he folded his hands behind his head. "Any ideas?"

An hour elapsed before Myaisha escorted him to the front door.

"Thank you, again," he said, buttoning up his bulky overcoat and slipping on gloves. "I appreciate the gift—and the fruit cake."

"Anytime."

She opened the door. "Merry Christmas and stop by any time." Myaisha climbed into boots and followed him outside.

"It's freezing." He secured the plastic container under his arm. He kissed her cheek. "Thanks for the cake. And Merry Christmas. Give Josiah my best."

Todd departed as AJ walked toward the house carrying a bouquet of roses.

Did AJ see Todd kiss her? Should she explain?

There wasn't anything to be embarrassed about. She and Todd were friends, completely innocent.

AJ shook hands with Todd, and they exchanged greetings. Myaisha watched Todd drive off.

After kissing her lips, AJ handed her the flowers. "Merry Christmas."

"Merry Christmas. Come in." Once inside, she removed her boots before following AJ into the living room.

Zoey rushed around their legs and up to Boomer. The dogs sniffed each other, then rushed down the hall to the secondary bedrooms.

"Would you like tea?"

"Sounds good."

AJ followed her into the kitchen. He came up behind her and hugged her around the waist. Myaisha stiffened her back and swung around.

Frowning, AJ asked, "What's wrong?"

Avoiding his question, Myaisha refilled the tea kettle and switched on the stove.

"Are we over?" AJ asked, swallowing hard.

Placing a hand on his chest, Myaisha lightly kissed him on the lips. AJ pulled her in close for a deep, passionate kiss.

He grinned. "It's like we're not connecting."

Circling around to the other side of the island, she asked, "Why do you say that?"

"Because you've been avoiding me."

"No, I haven't." She rested on a stool. "I simply didn't want to go to your place for Christmas."

With a deep sigh, AJ sat on a stool beside her. "Look, I know I'm clingy."

She smiled.

"You could disagree."

"Okay. You're not clingy, I simply need space."

"I understand."

The kettle whistled and she made their tea.

Once they settled together on the couch, AJ slipped a palm-size box from his breast pocket. "For you."

Excitedly, Myaisha unwrapped the package. She scrutinized it, unsure what it was. "Oh. Thank you."

AJ laughed. "It's a ring."

"I know that." She squinted at the silver ring. "But what is it? It looks like a hump."

"Turn it to the side." He took the ring and positioned it on its side. "See. It's a question mark."

"Neat." She frowned, turning the ring around repeatedly.

"Because you like mysteries."

Her eyes lit up. "I get it." She kissed his cheek. "It's sweet. Thank you."

"One day, when you're a successful writer, you can tell people this was your moment of inspiration."

Myaisha rose and retrieved a rectangular foot-long box. "For you."

AJ quickly tore apart the wrapping. "A tool belt."

"For your new business rehabbing houses."

He kissed her forehead. "How thoughtful."

Seated together on the couch, they sipped tea and discussed their past week.

"Maybe we can plan a weekend away in January," AJ said. "There's a new history—"

Myaisha stood and carried their mugs into the kitchen.

"What now?" AJ asked, following her.

"I told you I wanted space."

"January is—"

"It's not about that."

"Hell, Myaisha." He threw his hands up. "What is it about? Tell me."

Her nostrils flared. "Don't raise your voice."

"I…" He pivoted away and walked into the living room. "Help me understand. I'm trying to make this work."

"Maybe you shouldn't have to try so hard."

AJ winced. For a moment he stared at her, then whistled. Zoey raced up to him. He leashed the brown Lab, grabbed up his coat, and departed.

Boomer accompanied Zoey to the door. He whined as AJ took Zoey with him. The black Lab entered the kitchen and gazed up at her. He snorted and went to lie in the living room before the fireplace.

A beat later, Myaisha walked to the front door and locked it. She returned to the kitchen and began cleaning up. Frustrated, she threw the sponge in the sink and leaned against the refrigerator, uncertain how to fix the mess she'd created with AJ.

Tears trailed down her cheeks. A minute later, she started washing dishes.

CHAPTER 35

While the EHR booted up, Myaisha gazed out the back window of her medical office. From the corner of her eye, she looked at her cellphone. Twice last night she'd started to call AJ. Why couldn't she do it?

Things ended poorly on Christmas day—her fault. He had left his family party to be with her, and she had acted like a shrew. Truthfully, she didn't want to call him—not yet. Easier to avoid the topic for now. How long would AJ tolerate her indifferent behavior?

If she didn't want to be in a relationship with him, she should be up front. AJ deserved happiness, as did she. With a deep exhale, she rose and headed for patient room one.

Twenty minutes later, she completed the last morning appointment. Before she could exit the exam room, loud voices seeped under the door.

"Contact me if you experience any of the side effects we discussed," Myaisha said, escorting the patient toward the lobby.

"I want to speak with her now," Mr. Hopper demanded, slamming his palm on the reception countertop.

Slightly moving the patient behind her, Myaisha said, "Come over here, Mr. Hopper, where we can speak privately."

When he abandoned the reception desk, she whispered 'color purple' to Alma. The latter discretely picked up the desk phone.

While the front staff discharged patients, Myaisha led Mr. Hopper to the far corner of the lobby away from the reception desk. Quickly scanning the area, she verified no one was sitting nearby.

Mr. Hooper thrust a piece of paper into her face. "Explain this."

Myaisha disregarded the paper, instead observing Mr. Hopper's stance and the position of his hands. The self-defense training Grace provided their writing group came to mind.

Keep a safe distance. Look for a means of escape.

She said, "We mailed a formal notification to your home address. You can no longer receive medical care from our office—effective immediately."

"This is a threat. You told the medical board I assaulted a nurse," he huffed, darting the paper in front of her face. "I didn't touch that broad."

Once the other patients left the office, Myaisha squared her shoulders. "I suggest you leave right now. The police are on the way."

He snickered. "Listen to me, you quack. I'm not going anywhere until—"

"Leave now. We don't owe you an explanation, and none will be provided. If you don't understand the document, hire a lawyer to explain it."

Noticing his hands flinching, Myaisha stepped back with her right leg as her left hand fisted. Simultaneously,

Mr. Hopper charged forward. Before they connected, a gloved hand flew in front of her face and smacked the right side of Mr. Hopper's head.

Myaisha gasped.

In seconds, Dina had walloped Mr. Hopper and flipped him onto his buttocks.

Flustered and blubbering, he attempted to crawl off the floor. "You…How did you?"

Dina stepped on his neck. "Stay down," she said through clenched teeth.

Sirens wailed. Flashing lights dazzled inside the lobby.

Mr. Hopper squirmed, reaching up to grab Myaisha's ankle.

Stifled by a face mask, Dina said, "Don't move our I'll crush your throat."

His hand retreated and he lay on the floor as directed.

The gawking medical assistants pointed toward the scene as police rushed inside the medical office.

Over the next quarter of an hour, Myaisha detailed what had occurred. The police escorted Mr. Hopper, whose head drooped like a wilted plant, away and into their squad car. She accompanied them outside while providing details.

Once back inside the office, Myaisha locked the front door and collapsed into a lobby chair. The office staff joined her, but no one spoke.

Two minutes passed before Alma said, "Dina, I'm sorry—"

"We're sorry," Yvette said, glancing at both medical assistants, "about teasing you."

"Where did you learn to flip a man like that?" Shirley asked.

"After…" Dina stared at the floor.

Though tempted to hug the nurse, Myaisha respected her space.

"I won't be a victim again," Dina said, observing her trembling, gloved hands.

"Well, we handled the situation together." Myaisha glanced at Alma. "You understood the color purple code."

"We've trained on hostile situations," Yvette said.

"The most important thing is for us to function as a team. We need to support each other." Myaisha surveyed the staff, giving each person an extra second of attention. "This shouldn't simply be an office where we work. I want this to be a home where we care for people. A place where you and our patients can be safe. We need to come together as a unit to make that happen."

Each person nodded in agreement.

Having dismissed the staff, Myaisha retired to her office to chart and complete quarterly reports. She jotted a note to contact the state medical board again about Mr. Hopper's inappropriate and increasingly aggressive behavior. Though they provided instructions on dismissing unruly patients, she wanted guidance on filing a civil restraint. Maybe she should call her lawyer.

Boom, boom.

The sudden noise made Myaisha jump in her seat. Deniece stood at the window, signaling her to open the door.

Heart racing, Myaisha unlocked the rear door. "You frightened me."

"Why so jumpy?"

"What are you doing here?" she asked.

Deniece slid out of her winter coat and sat in front of Myaisha's desk. "I'm hungry. Want to grab lunch?"

"You could have called."

"What's wrong with dropping by. You're done seeing patients, aren't you?"

"Yes." Myaisha shut down her computer. "But after today's events, I was a little startled."

"Today's events." Deniece exited the office behind her. "What's been going on?"

"I'll tell you in the car."

Inside Deniece's SUV, Myaisha reclined against the head rest and closed her eyes.

"Are you going to tell me or take a nap?"

"Remember the patient I told you about who assaulted Dina?"

"Uh huh."

Myaisha rubbed her eyes. "Well, he came back after receiving the dismissal letter."

Deniece snuck a glance at her between observing traffic. "I presume he didn't come back to apologize."

"For the Cliff Notes version, Dina smacked him in the head and dropped him like a rock."

Deniece gaped. "No."

"Yes, ma'am." Myaisha sat up straight. "Timid Dina is more like a tigress."

"I thought she had it in her."

She glanced at her friend.

"Don't mess with a nurse. We know how to inflict pain."

"Not exactly the moniker for a healthcare advertisement."

"No, but a growing concern with hospital violence rising."

"True."

Should she consider security cameras? The privacy of her staff would diminish. A camera wouldn't have helped in the situation with Mr. Hopper.

"Should I buy a gun for the office?"

Deniece's forehead creased. "Are you allowed to have a weapon in a medical office?"

"Another thing to ask the medical board." And she would definitely call her lawyer.

CHAPTER 36

Conversation around the department ebbed and flowed like the tide. One moment silence, the next Todd couldn't hear his own thoughts.

What should he do next?

Hovering over his office desk, Todd gazed blankly.

"Are you going to stand there all day like a sad puppy?" Ian asked, chewing on a burrito.

He glared at his partner. "I was considering whether to review witness statements or conduct more interviews."

"Consider the options while sitting." Ian tossed the empty wrapper into the trash. "You look crazy standing their moping."

Though he hadn't reached a decision, Todd decided to sit.

"What did the chief say?"

"Come back when you have more." Todd sighed and turned on his desktop computer.

"He didn't mention arresting Lowry?"

"Not this time. I convinced him it wouldn't look good to arrest a widowed mother of three during the holidays."

"Dude, she's got the best motive and weakest alibi."

"Too easy." He reviewed where he'd left off with his documentation and started typing. "Did she strike you as stupid?"

"She didn't act like a rocket scientist." Ian chugged a pint of orange juice. "Any fresh ideas?"

"Ms. Creighton had access to the poison. Forensics located the substance in her office kitchenette."

"But why would she keep SMFA in the office kitchen?"

"Exactly." Todd wrapped his fingers behind his head and gazed up at the ceiling.

"Someone set her up."

"That's what I think."

"But why frame her for murder if they planned to kill her?"

A moment passed as Todd reflected. "Two separate killers. One murdered Mr. Lowry, the other Ms. Creighton."

Ian said, "She made a perfect suspect. Means and motive."

"Myaisha said Ms. Creighton truly loved Mr. Lowry."

"People have killed their loved ones before."

"Ms. Creighton was attractive and successful. She could have walked away from the relationship." Todd typed his report.

"You place a lot of stock in what the doctor believes."

"She understands people, and she's a snoop. If I can't keep her away from my investigation, why not benefit from her efforts?"

Chuckling, Ian said, "Y'all like each other. Get a room and consummate things."

Shooting his partner a glare, he said, "Not today. I'm not in the mood."

An hour passed.

"I emailed you my report," Ian said, stretching. "Let me know what you think."

"Give me a moment," Todd said, considering how to spell a word.

Returning from the vending machine, Ian asked, "What about the tapes?"

"Shush," Todd said, glancing around the station.

Ian lowered his voice. "Are you going to tell the captain?"

"Not if they aren't relevant."

Propping his feet on the desk, Ian said, "They might be the motive. Lowry might have used incriminating tapes of their rendezvous for blackmail."

"For which murder?" His fingers tapped on the desktop as if along piano keys. "But Lowry couldn't release them without also compromising himself."

Ian chomped on chips. "Creighton might not have wanted her family learning about her kinky side."

Todd shook his head. "Daddy is dead, and Ms. Creighton had been well set financially. Her family had no control over her. On the other hand, Mr. Lowry had more to lose. Once he lost his job and reputation, what were the odds a judge would give him sole custody of the kids?"

"The wife is also on the tapes."

"But technically she didn't commit adultery. The neighbors said he'd been verbally abusive. He might have forced her into the activity."

"We need to speak with her."

He checked his watch. "She keeps putting it off."

Ian picked up the phone. "I'll insist." A minute later he hung up. "Goes directly to voicemail."

"Guess we'll have to drive out there." The kids would certainly be home, but Mrs. Lowry had to be interviewed again. *I hate this case.*

"So, what are you going to do with the tapes?" Ian asked before guzzling orange juice.

"Keep them off the record until we determine if they're relevant." He reviewed Ian's report and a minute later mumbled, "No need to destroy innocent people."

"Who would frame Creighton for murder?" Ian asked between bites of the burrito. "Then murder her?"

"That is a mystery," Todd said, while emailing his report to the captain. "I keep getting the same answer." He looked across the desk at his partner.

"The wife."

"I hope we're wrong, or three kids will lose both their parents."

"Not our problem. If she's a murderer, they need to be protected."

His shoulders slumped. "What a lousy Christmas."

CHAPTER 37

Scents of cumin and cardamon welcomed them inside the restaurant. Myaisha chose a table with a window view. The waitstaff took their order and filled their water glasses.

"So, Dina turned out to be a dynamo," Deniece said, sipping water.

Myaisha chewed on naan. "I'm proud of her. She stood up for herself."

"Are the staff behaving?"

"They won't be teasing Dina anymore."

"Now they know she can whoop their butts."

Their laughter petered out to a pleasant silence.

Touching Myaisha's hand, Deniece asked, "Have you called AJ?"

She shook her head, avoiding her friend's gaze. "Not yet."

"What are you waiting for?"

"I'm not sure I'm sorry about what happened."

Deniece's eyes widened.

Neither spoke until the waitstaff stepped away.

"Do you love him?"

"That's not it." Myaisha ate. She didn't want to discuss AJ.

"Okay." Deniece leaned back in the seat and consumed her meal. "Clearly, we aren't talking about relationships today."

Deniece pointed at Myaisha's hand. "What's that?"

Myaisha splayed her fingers to better display the ring. "A Christmas gift from AJ."

Deniece frowned. "But what is the design?"

Sliding the ring off her finger, Myaisha handed it over. "A question mark. Turn it on its side."

Deniece did as instructed. "Oh, now I see it."

She replaced the ring on her finger. "It's because I write mysteries."

"How sweet," Deniece said, her eyes twinkling.

"Fine." Myaisha wiped her mouth and slid the plate aside. "Let's talk about my failing relationship. I'm irritated with AJ. He—"

"Adores you. Pampers you with affection. Gives you nice gifts with sentimental attachments." Deniece ticked the items off her fingers. "Oh my. Such an irritating boyfriend."

"Forget it." Myaisha checked her watch. "I've got patients waiting." She dropped two twenties on the table and departed.

"Hey," Deniece said, hurrying after her, "I'm your ride. Keep the attitude to yourself."

Inside the car, Myaisha said, "Sorry. I...I'm not ready to talk about this."

"With me or AJ?"

"Anyone."

As she pulled around the rear of the bungalow Myaisha had converted into a medical office, Deniece said, "Be careful. Don't lose a good man because you can't address your feelings."

"Thanks for the support."

"I can't carry you through this." Deniece placed the car in park and turned to face her. "It's been a while since your last relationship, but the steps are the same. Mutual kindness and respect." She placed a hand on Myaisha's knee. "If you don't want to be with AJ, tell him. Be direct. He deserves the truth."

Barely nodding for fear the tears in her eyes would pour down her face, Myaisha exited the car and returned to her office.

Chapter 38

Hearing the garage door raise, Myaisha set down the clothes hamper and entered the garage. "Josiah?"

"Hey, Mom."

Boomer scampered outside and circled the blue ten-speed bike.

"Where are you going?" She shivered and regarded her house shoes. "It's cold out here."

"Fifty degrees isn't bad," he said, slipping the helmet over his head.

"Maybe. But with the wind, it feels like thirty. Don't you want a larger jacket?"

"Sure."

He climbed off the bike and followed her inside.

Myaisha finished the laundry while Josiah retrieved a more substantial coat.

"This better," he said, posing for her as if modeling.

She smacked his arm. "I don't need the sarcasm. I simply want you to be warm—and safe."

"I know, Mom." He gave her a hug. "I'm not a child."

She smiled but didn't answer, as she admired the man he had become.

"Be back in an hour."

"If not, Boomer and I will come looking for you."

The Lab barked. Josiah petted his head. "What's wrong?"

"Nothing. Another crazy day at work." She put on a jacket and followed him into the garage. "Does your headlamp work? I hate it when you ride at night."

"It's fine." He clicked it on. "See."

Myaisha scrutinized the bike. "The tires need air."

"They're fine."

Josiah biked to the edge of the driveway before cycling back. "Don't get mad, but you should call AJ and apologize."

She frowned, resting a hand on her hip. "What do you mean?"

"Mom, I overhead your conversation on Christmas." He strapped on the helmet. "Since I've been home, I've noticed how you treat him and the cop. You've been acting like a teenage girl. Playing come here, now go."

"I…" She struggled with defending herself and chastising him for criticizing her relationships.

"If you want to be with the detective, let AJ go. He seems like a nice guy."

"My affairs are none of your business."

With his shoe, Josiah twirled the peddles. "And you wonder why we don't discuss sensitive issues like relationships."

"I'm always open to discussing anything you want."

"Except *your* personal affairs."

Myaisha bristled.

"If you want us to move beyond the mother-child bond, talk to me like an adult."

"One introductory psychology class and you're psychoanalyzing our attachment."

"After dad died, it was only the two of us for years. We know each other's weaknesses and fears." He leaned over and kissed her cheek. "I want you to be happy. If AJ makes you happy, don't let him go because you're afraid."

With that pronouncement, Josiah cycled away.

Boomer's whining reminded her they were standing in a cold garage. Inside, she tossed him a treat and returned to cleaning.

How dare Josiah speak to her that way. As his mother, she deserved respect. But objecting to her son's statement wouldn't hide the truth. She had been harsh with AJ, treated their affection with indifference. Since their trip to Charlotte, she had been pushing him away. Had she been using her friendship with Todd as a wedge?

She understood how AJ regarded their relationship. Dangling Todd in front of him had been an adolescent gesture. Myaisha plopped on the couch and stretched out her legs. If she cared for him, she should apologize.

For a long moment, she gazed at the ring AJ had given her for Christmas. He truly believed she could become a published author. He encouraged her. Listened to her story ideas despite the fact he hated mysteries.

Though she considered long and hard, Myaisha couldn't identify one objectionable characteristic in her boyfriend—except he was clingy. But she appreciated his attention. Smiling, she gazed down at the ring.

Call him.

She rose and searched for her cellphone. Before dialing, an idea sprung into her mind. The cellphone hung limply in her hand.

When it rang, Myaisha startled and dropped it. The screen read AJ. Not now.

In the foyer, she layered up in a scarf, gloves, and coat. The cellphone went to voicemail as she departed.

CHAPTER 39

The quiet cul-de-sac represented quintessential Americana. Families drove SUVs with their children and dogs to soccer and football games. Several houses sported patriotic flags. Two homes still had Christmas lights on.

Myaisha noticed front porch lights on in a half dozen homes. Families gathered together, either having dinner or viewing television. Though more likely than not, the families were scattered around the house, eating food alone and watching television in their individual rooms.

Myaisha had never been a person to cherish the past. People who decried the present in admiration of America's past were often wishing for a time where they had security as the dominant force in society.

However, Christmas made her desire the past. Josiah as a child, mesmerized by the magic of the holidays as they curled up together on the couch drinking hot chocolate in front of the fireplace.

Sammy. As the years grew since his death, Myaisha recalled fewer memories of her deceased husband. She had loved him dearly. His death had sent her spiraling into a catatonic depression. If not for her responsibilities as a mother… Even then, her family had to support her for that first year.

From the moment they met in college until his precipitous death, she and Sammy were never apart for more than a week. A medical conference, a girl's weekend. Those few brief moments separated them over the more than twenty years of their relationship.

Then it ended.

Myaisha's breath caught. The cold air stung her throat. She hurried down the street and knocked on her neighbor's door.

"Well, Myaisha. What brings you out this evening?"

"May I come in?"

"Of course."

Warmth enveloped Myaisha, and her shoulders relaxed. "Sorry about the timing. Is your husband home?"

Abigail led her into the living room. Myaisha followed the wheelchair.

"Roger is with his friends, bowling."

She smiled. "I used to bowl."

"So did I." Abigail wheeled herself next to the fireplace. "Not anymore."

The logs crinkled in the blazing fireplace. "That's quite a fire." Myaisha bent down, peering into the hearth. "Would you like me to help you over to the couch?"

"I can do it myself," Abigail said archly.

"Sorry." Myaisha sat down and waited until Abigail situated herself next to the couch.

"How can I help you?" Abigail asked, folding her hands on her lap.

Sliding forward on her chair, Myaisha said, "You have the most delicate hands."

Abigail blushed. "Thank you."

"I admired them the other day when Josiah and I dropped off the Christmas gifts. They caught my attention as you wheeled into the living room." Myaisha held Abigail's gaze.

"How observant." The latter discretely slid her hands under the throw covering her legs.

"If you remember, Roger and I picked up an item off the floor when it dropped beside the wheelchair. For a brief moment, we bumped into each other, and he knocked me up against your legs. Strong, firm legs." Her gaze bore into Abigail's face as she placed a slight emphasis on the last sentence.

Abigail threw back her shoulders, holding her head high. "I thought you needed something. This isn't a good time for reminiscences. I need to rest."

"How long has your multiple sclerosis been in remission?"

Flinching, Abigail said, "It's not."

Myaisha reclined into the chair. "I noticed the ring."

Quizzically regarding her, Abigail asked, "What ring?"

Extending her hand, Myaisha pointed to the ring AJ had given her for Christmas. "From my boyfriend." She slid it off her finger and handed it to Abigail. "At first, I couldn't understand what it symbolized."

Abigail cautiously accepted it. "And what is it?"

"If you turn it to the side, you'll see it's a question mark."

"Oh, yes. Now it's clear."

Holding out her hand, Myaisha waited for Abigail to return the ring. The latter surrendered it reluctantly.

"Forgive me, but I don't understand. Did you come over to show me your Christmas gift?"

Myaisha observed Abigail's puffy skin under deeply mascaraed eyes. "I don't recall seeing you wear such heavy makeup before. Are you celebrating or grieving?"

Arching her back, Abigail rolled the wheelchair toward the foyer. "Forgive me, but I must ask you to leave. This conversation—"

"Can remain between us," Myaisha said craning her neck to view Abigail in the foyer, "or I can call Detective Gamble."

"Humph." Abigail slowly returned to the living room. "Your boyfriend."

Myaisha's shoulders bristled. "He's not..." She exhaled. "Don't get off topic."

Raising a crooked brow, Abigail asked, "Which is?"

"You killed Jared and Sharon."

Abigail's weak guffaw sounded awkward in the quiet domesticated home. A flush rose up her chest and covered her neck. "Reading mysteries has led you to confuse fantasy with reality. What an absurd accusation."

"I don't make it lightly." Myaisha moved to the couch beside Abigail. "It must have taken an extreme amount of rage to shoot Sharon in the head. Poisoning Jared required stealth."

For minutes, the chiming clock created the single noise in the entire house. Myaisha watched Abigail, who stared into the flames.

"You have no proof."

"It can be found."

Her shoulders sank, as Abigail's chin trembled. "I won't hurt Roger."

"He doesn't have to know."

With a suspicious glance, Abigail asked, "How could it be kept secret?"

"If you confessed, explained how you did it," Myaisha's shoulders shrugged, "I'm sure the police would be content."

"Roger wouldn't accept it."

"The innocent must be protected."

"Innocent." Abigail cackled. "No one involved in this affair is innocent."

"There's a big leap from infidelity to murder."

"Is there?" Abigail asked, plucking at the fabric in the throw.

A moment elapsed before Myaisha said, "Your ring gave it away."

Abigail raised her hand. "This ring."

She nodded. "Jared gave it to you, didn't he?"

Grinning, Abigail climbed out of the wheelchair and joined Myaisha on the couch. Like a gossiping teen, she showed her the ring.

"Our little secret. Roger thought it represented waves, but it's actually the number sixty-nine." Abigail winked suggestively. "Our favorite position."

Myaisha winced.

This time, Abigail laughed long and heartily. "Oh, Myaisha. Don't play naïve with me. I've seen you with your cop and fireman."

"It's not what you think." Her jaw tensed.

"Oh." Abigail's lips puckered. "Are you going to pretend innocence like Patsy? Poor pathetic Patsy. Little fool."

Myaisha regarded the neighbor she had associated with for almost twenty years—unable to recognize the woman she had invited into her home and her life. Family dinners and other activities together with Abigail and Roger, before and after Sammy died.

"Have you no compassion for her?"

"Did you have any for Jared?"

Ashamed, Myaisha closed her mouth. When she learned about Jared's death, she had no compassion for him, nor interest in the incident. In fact, she believed he deserved it. But she would atone for her sins later.

"Was this about the videos or money?"

Abigail crossed her legs, extending her arm along the back of the couch. "I wasn't stupid enough to let him film me."

"He did it anonymously."

Nodding, Abigail said, "He threatened to show the videos to Roger."

"How did it start? I mean…you're sophisticated, classy. But Jared dressed like a slouch and acted like a pig."

"Yes, but he was one hundred percent male," Abigail said in a breathy voice. "Which was all I needed from him. Pure ecstasy."

Perhaps noticing Myaisha's questioning brows, Abigail continued.

"Roger loves me." She tossed her hair back. "But he placed me on a pedestal and protected me." Abigail sighed. "I'm a woman not a China doll."

Placing a hand on Abigail's forearm, she asked, "Why didn't you talk to him? Explain your needs, how you missed the passion in your relationship."

Abigail snatched her arm away. "I did." She strode around the living room.

A pang of guilt stung Myaisha. She hadn't been up front with AJ about her emotions. How could she fault Abigail?

"So many times I explained to Roger how I felt, what I needed—wanted. In various ways I told him, showed him, I was a woman."

She giggled. "I even walked around the house butt naked. Roger would carry me to my bedroom and place me in bed, go to the guest bedroom, and leave me there alone."

"Then why pretend you needed a wheelchair?"

"Being a China doll is better than being ignored."

"And the separate bedrooms?"

A crooked grin crossed Abigail's mouth. "Roger's idea, because of his sleep apnea. It made things easier though. At night, Jared would slip inside my bedroom window. Roger couldn't hear anything over his CPAP machine."

"The videos."

"Blackmail. Jared needed money."

"And poison."

"I dressed as a gardener and slipped out my bedroom window. One afternoon, I exited onto a side street and simply walked over to his house. Sprinkled the SMFA inside three water bottles." Abigail perched on the edge of a chair.

"Jared had always been a smug—arrogant cad. The day of the murder, I donned a gardener outfit and paid him a visit. He was surprised, but not suspicious. He always drank water while working out in the garage. I collected the videos and waited for the poison to kick in."

"What if the kids drank from one of the water bottles instead?"

"Would it have been such a loss?"

Myaisha gasped. "How reckless."

"Those kids are future psychopaths."

Amazing when you learn what your neighbors truly think about people.

"Don't get me wrong," Abigail said hurriedly. "I adore kids—just not brats like Jared's brood."

"I see," Myaisha said softly.

"Josiah is a wonderful son." Abigail sat on the couch beside her. "You deserve the credit. Handsome and strong. Roger and I have watched him mature. Sammy would've been proud."

Though she admired the praise, Myaisha had no intention of discussing her son at that moment.

"A delivery driver died because of you."

Abigail's forehead wrinkled. "Yes. An unfortunate occurrence. It's hard to account for all possibilities."

"And Sharon became another one of those *unfortunate* events?"

Her eyes mere slits, Abigail glared at Myaisha. "She called me. Threatened to tell Roger about my involvement with Jared."

"Sharon learned about you and Jared?"

"Apparently, he told her." Abigail frowned. "The bastard."

"And how did you expect to get away with this?"

Sitting up straight, Abigail gazed into her face. "No one knows but you."

A thrill shot up Myaisha's spine, momentary fear. However, she regarded Abigail's pleading face and understood.

"I can't keep this secret."

"Why not?" Abigail asked, grasping her arm. "I won't kill anyone else. Promise."

The absurdity of that statement was clearly lost on Abigail. Myaisha pried her arm loose, aware of the present danger.

"Innocent people died."

"Jared abused his wife and raised a trio of juvenile delinquents. He blackmailed Tiffany and Carter and committed adultery with Sharon."

"Does that justify murder—three murders?"

"Who'll miss them?" Abigail shrieked.

"And the delivery driver?"

Abigail turned away and circled the living room again. "I apologized."

"To his family?"

She whirled around. "What do you expect me to do?"

"Confess."

"And cleanse my soul." Abigail strode around the room again. "I'm afraid there is no god I pray to for forgiveness."

"This is why people shouldn't be judge and jury." Myaisha rose. "I wanted to give you a chance."

In a second, Abigail rushed in front of her, blocking any egress. Myaisha raised her hands defensively.

Fast moves, for a person claiming to require a wheelchair due to multiple sclerosis.

"Are you going to kill me too?"

Abigail's chest rose and fell. "Please. I simply wanted to protect Roger. If he discovered the truth, it would break his heart. He truly loves me."

"People loved Jared, and Sharon, and the delivery driver."

Abigail's body trembled.

"How far will you go to keep a secret?"

The women stared at each other. At the hour, the clock struck and broke the impasse.

"Tomorrow, I call the homicide detectives."

Her eyes wide and wild, Abigail clutched Myaisha's wrist. "I won't let anyone hurt Roger. I won't."

Peeling herself free, she said, "You should have considered the consequences before you let Jared into your bed. All this misery could have been avoided."

Abigail's face scrunched up. She hurled the words at Myaisha. "So high and mighty. Don't judge me. One day my life is perfect. Roger and I were active, traveling, socializing with friends. Then came multiple sclerosis."

"A serious illness disrupted your life."

"It changed my husband more than it did me." She glowered at Myaisha. "I couldn't walk, could barely move for the first year. Roger stayed by my side every moment of each day."

"He loves you."

Tears wet Abigail's face. "When I recovered, he had forgotten the old Abigail."

"Roger feared he might lose you."

"He lost me to his fear, not the disease."

Sobbing, Abigail pleaded. "Don't destroy his idea of this Abigail."

"Don't blame me. You created this situation. You forgot the old Roger."

As Abigail cried uncontrollably, snot and tears streamed down her neck. "I won't let you hurt him."

"If you had cared more about Roger's feelings, you wouldn't have invited Jared into your bed."

Myaisha pivoted around and exited, conscious all the time of Abigail's eyes on her back. Though she recognized the need for prudence, Abigail had not been a spontaneous killer—yet.

Outside, Myaisha hurried home, not wanting to tempt fate.

CHAPTER 40

Minutes became hours. Time sped by. Myaisha sat on the edge of her bed, tired from twisting and turning all night. She had slept little.

Yesterday evening, she'd spoken boldly about going to the authorities and being able to obtain proof of Abigail's guilt. First, she would have to explain to Todd what occurred last night. He would be furious, but she could fabricate an excuse. If she had contacted him last night, he might have arrested Abigail immediately and without proof…

But that's not why she had delayed informing Todd. Last night Abigail had called, begging for a chance to protect Roger. Myaisha hoped that Abigail had explained to Roger what had transpired so he wouldn't find out from the police.

Myaisha secretly wished Abigail would confess and she wouldn't have to get involved with a prolonged investigation. She got up and dressed; being late for work wouldn't help.

Once she fed Boomer, Myaisha grabbed her coat and Irish walking hat and departed. As the garage doors scrolled up, red and blue lights bounced off the walls. Her shoulders tensed. Like a person in a trance, she walked out of the garage and gazed across the cul-de-sac. Five police vehicles were parked in Abigail's driveway.

Had Abigail murdered Roger to keep her affair secret?

Nauseated, Myaisha covered her mouth.

Last night, she had considered informing Todd about her discovery, but Abigail begged her not to do anything before morning. Myaisha had promised.

Now she feared a desperate, Abigail might have killed Roger to preserve his memory of her as a devoted, dutiful wife. If keeping the videotapes secret upset Todd, discovering she'd solved the murders before he had would make him furious. If her silence had led to Roger's death…

At a crawl, Myaisha drove by the Tipton's house. She caught Todd's eye. His head moved slowly from side to side. Her stomach did a somersault. He waved her over. Grasping the steering wheel with one hand, she rolled down the window.

His grim face spoke volumes.

"I'm afraid to ask."

"Mrs. Tipton."

"Yes," she asked, watching his lips.

"Dead."

"Oh, no!"

Roger killed Abigail! She hadn't suspected. Her hands trembled. "How?"

"She took an overdose."

"What?" Myaisha frowned. "I don't understand."

"We need a statement from all the neighbors."

"Of course."

"I'll be over shortly."

She executed a U-turn and reentered the garage. As she came inside the house, Boomer's head cocked to the side and an ear raised.

"I know." Myaisha removed her coat. "Mommy's back early."

Anticipating Todd's arrival, she unlocked the front door and removed the dead bolt. She opened the door, intending to leave it ajar, but an envelope dropped on her shoe. Absently shutting the door, Myaisha sat on the couch and read the missive.

***

A half hour later, Todd poked his head in the door.

"Myaisha?"

Boomer barked and hustled into the foyer. The door slammed closed.

Opening the door, Myaisha invited Todd inside. He peered around her cautiously.

"Where's Cujo?"

"If you want Boomer to love you, stop calling him names."

"I don't need his love, only his promise not to eat me."

"Don't be dramatic."

"Says the woman whose dog could rip out my throat."

"Boomer wouldn't be so scary if you became his friend."

He followed her into the living room. His gaze scanned the floor for the Lab. "We don't need to be friends."

"Lemonade?" She didn't wait for a reply, knowing he would answer affirmatively.

Todd spotted Boomer in the kitchen. "I'm good here."

"Boomer, go."

The Lab skirted in front of Todd, sniffing his feet and snorting before resting in front of the rear sliding glass doors.

Once the Lab lay down, Todd sat on a stool at the kitchen island. Myaisha placed a glass of lemonade and a plate of cookies in front of him.

"Where's Josiah?" Todd asked before sipping his lemonade.

Myaisha glanced down the hallway. "He left for school this morning."

Todd scooped up a cookie. "Did you expect Mrs. Tipton to commit suicide?"

"Of course not!"

Boomer scurried off the floor and headed for Todd.

Myaisha came around the island and met Boomer. "Mommy's sorry. It's okay." She petted the Lab and retired to the living room.

From the safety of the kitchen, Todd said, "I noticed your expression in the car."

"I…" She held out the letter. "Read this."

Making a large arc around Boomer, Todd accepted the paper and read it.

Myaisha rubbed Boomer's back while observing Todd's reaction.

"This is significantly different than the note she wrote at the house."

"Care to share?" Myaisha asked, gesturing for him to be seated.

Sitting lightly on the edge of the couch, Todd kept an eye on the Lab. "Her suicide note read she had killed

Mr. Lowry because he abused his wife and kids. Ms. Creighton attempted to blackmail her, which led to the third death. And the delivery driver, of course, had been accident."

Nodding, Myaisha reached for the letter. Todd withheld it. Her forehead creased. "Abigail meant that for my eyes only."

"It's evidence."

"I trusted you with her secret."

They stared at each other.

"Why do you need it?" She rose and approached him. "You have a confession and a solution to the murders."

"She didn't murder three people out of altruism."

Her shoulders slumped. "No, she didn't. But does Roger have to be hurt? She wanted me to protect him."

"The truth will set you free." A tiny curl danced at the corner of his lip.

"Sometimes truth hurts, often it leads to worse problems." When she reached for the letter this time, he released it. "Thank you."

"The delivery driver's family deserves closure."

"And they'll have it." She folded the letter and placed it inside the envelope. "They will know who killed their loved one. The true motive for his death won't matter to the family. Truth will not resurrect the man."

Todd slumped on to the couch. "All this for a booty call."

"The murders involved more than sex. Abigail killed to preserve her respectability."

She sat on the other couch. "People fight for freedom and independence but scorn it in regard to sex."

"Is sex worth throwing away your life?"

"Carter probably hadn't considered running for political office when he and Tiffany initiated their relationship with Jared and Patsy." She gazed at the ceiling. "Young people can't see beyond the moment."

Todd swallowed the remaining lemonade. "Years pass and priorities change."

"Absolutely."

He placed the glass in the kitchen sink, scooping up the remaining cookies. "Have your interests changed?" He walked up to her.

Myaisha froze, unsure if his question held a double entendre. Though he stood not a foot away, she appreciated a more substantial distance between them. In addition to being older than him by at least ten years, Todd didn't appeal to her in the way AJ did. They shared common interests in mysteries, puzzles, and criminology, but she couldn't see herself romantically involved with him.

"You all right?" he asked, lightly touching her forearm.

"Yes, thank you." She led him to the foyer. "So much has happened."

"What's that?" he asked, pointing to her ring.

"A gift from AJ." Answering the question in his eyes, she quickly said, "It's a question mark."

Todd held her hand, scrutinizing the ring. He released her hand. "Clever."

At the door, he swung around. They nearly bumped their heads.

"He's a good guy."

At the door, Myaisha watched him walk away. *Did he mean that honestly?* It didn't matter.

In the kitchen, she lit the stove gas burner and watched Abigail's letter disintegrate.

Chapter 41

The Christmas tree remained in the corner of the detectives' office, but its lights were muted. Todd wondered how long it would take for someone to pack it away. Last year, it remained in the corner until St. Patrick's Day. Todd typed the last sentence of his report then used spell-check to scan for errors.

"Are you done yet?" Ian asked, gathering documents together into a manila folder.

"Hold on." Todd scanned the report once more. "What's your hurry?"

"I'm hungry." Ian slid the folder across their desks. Todd caught it before it crashed on the floor.

"You're always hungry."

"Yeah, well you ate your fair share of ham and paella on Christmas day."

"A compliment to your mom's delicious cooking." Todd rose. "I sent the report to the printer. Should be ready in a few minutes."

"Good. I can't wait to close this case."

Five minutes later, Todd returned with the printed document and stuffed it into the manila folder. "Done. Want to drop it off now or after lunch?"

Ian checked his watch. "After. Let's go, before the sandwich shop gets busy."

As they exited the police station, Todd said, "We can always go down the street. Green Pastures Café has delicious soups, and you'll like their sandwiches."

"Sure, why not."

Once they crossed over Greene Street, Ian asked, "What did you do with the videotapes?"

"Incinerator."

"Seriously?"

Todd shrugged. "With Mrs. Tipton's confession to both murders in the suicide note, there's no reason to drag the Stilwells' alternative lifestyle into the spotlight."

Ian held the café door open. "You're a softy."

"Screw you."

"That was the problem with this case. Too many people screwing the wrong people."

"Not funny."

Grinning, Ian said, "It's a little funny."

They approached the register and placed their orders. Todd set the stand with their order number in the center of the table. Ian guzzled his soda.

"So, you going to ask the doctor out?"

"Don't go there." Todd gazed out the window at passing traffic.

"Dude, it's okay. Many guys like older women—not me—but it's not unusual."

"Back off."

"Touchy." Ian grinned. "That means it's a sensitive issue."

"I don't like her in that way."

The server brought their meals in to-go bags. As they departed, Ian hummed the song, "And he says she's just a friend."

Todd threw a pickle at him. "Not Biz Markie again."

They left the café with Ian singing off tune, and Todd trying not to listen.

However, he recognized Myaisha had become more than a friend. Presently, things between them were copacetic. Unless something happened, or she asked for more, he would be content with their current circumstance.

CHAPTER 42

Conversations filled the hallway of Myaisha's medical office, separating patient exam rooms from the nursing station. She rushed from the exam room into her private office. Yvette followed.

"Call the ER," she said, giving orders while searching her desk drawers. "Tell them—"

"What are you looking for?" Yvette asked.

"The number for the oncologist in Raleigh."

"I have it, Mrs. Doctor." Yvette pulled the number up on the EHR.

"Good tell them…"

Morning clinic ended in a whirl of patients and orders. Myaisha returned to her desk at around one o'clock in the afternoon. She had packed a peanut butter and jelly sandwich for lunch but had no appetite.

Closing her door, she unfurled an exercise mat and completed several yoga stretches. Fifteen minutes into the exercises, her neck eventually relaxed. She could even look over her shoulder. *Maybe I should cut back on office hours.*

Now less tense, her appetite returned, and she munched on a sandwich while making phone calls. "Hello, D."

"What's up? It's too late to grab lunch."

"I'm calling about our Friday card game."

"You cancelling again."

"Sorry."

"Why? Todd got another performance."

"That's not the reason."

"Then why?"

"I need—"

"You're avoiding AJ aren't you?"

"No, I'm not," she said, aware of her defensive tone.

"Fine. No card game on Friday. But you're making a mistake with AJ."

"I'm doing what's best for me." Myaisha hung up. She didn't want to hear a lecture, not even from her best friend.

CHAPTER 43

Lightly squeezing Roger's hand, Myaisha scanned the room. A life-size picture of Abigail perched near the hallway entrance. Flower arrangements graced every available surface, creating an overpowering scent of spring.

But it was winter, and a frosty quietness encapsulated the house. Visitors streamed by offering Roger condolences.

Myaisha gave him a final hug. "Let me know if you need anything." She pivoted to leave, but Roger held her hand.

"Thank you." He palmed her hand in both of his. "You and Sammy." Tears welled in Roger's eyes. "Josiah." He cleared his throat. "Abigail and I always appreciated neighbors like you."

He glanced beyond her. Myaisha noticed Patsy enter.

"Jared was a thug." His shoulders tensed. "Abigail and I detested him." He looked into her eyes. "We talked about how poorly he treated his family, but I never imagined…"

He coughed and blew his nose.

"Abigail had always put other people first. What it took for her to protect Patsy." He shook his head. "A saint, my Abigail."

A guest approached. Myaisha used the opportunity to escape. For the present, she had heard enough about saint Abigail. Patsy waylaid her at the door.

"I wasn't sure about paying my respects." Patsy lowered her voice. "Does he blame me?"

Myaisha removed Patsy's hand from her arm. "He will appreciate your stopping by."

"It's hard to believe." Patsy started toward the crowd surrounding Roger. "Abigail did this for me and the kids."

Observing the mother of three, Myaisha wondered if Patsy feigned naivety or simply lacked common sense. Either way, she and the kids would get a fresh start with the insurance money. And Jared *had* been a horrid husband.

Were the kids coping? They had issues before their father's death. This would not improve things.

Outside, Myaisha dashed to her house, aware of the cold, and tired from the exhausting day. On the way, Tiffany called.

Scampering outside in shorts and a bomber jacket, Tiffany said, "So, you paid your respects to the dearly departed angelic Abigail."

"Don't be snide." Myaisha started to depart but pivoted around. "She got you off the hook."

Wide eyed, Tiffany said, "You don't believe we were involved."

"I know you weren't. But if Abigail hadn't confessed, the police would have continued their investigation."

Straightening her back, Tiffany strode up to her face. "You aren't...Did you keep those tapes?"

Returning the glare, Myaisha asked, "Do you believe I would blackmail you and Carter?"

Tiffany stepped back. "No. I'm sorry. This whole thing has been surreal."

"And more so for Roger."

Nodding, Tiffany said, "He really believes she was a saint."

"He's a kind man. Let him have his fantasy."

"No woman wants to be placed on a pedestal and admired."

"Some might." Myaisha strode off before Tiffany could respond.

Inside the house, she had barely removed her coat when the doorbell rang. Myaisha's face lit up. "Oh, hello, Mrs. Lula."

The septuagenarian entered at her invitation.

"How was your trip?"

"Short. May I have my key back?" she asked curtly.

"Sure. Come in. I have it in the pantry."

"Interesting place to keep it," Mrs. Lula said, following her closely.

"A place no one would consider, and where I spend a lot of time."

The neighbor did not return her smile. *What is going on with Mrs. Lula?*

"Everything okay?"

"Yeah," Mrs. Lula said, grabbing the key. "Any problems? Did you have to go inside?"

"Well…" Myaisha paused, aware of the increased attention from her neighbor. "Let's sit down and I'll explain."

"Can't. Got stuff to do."

"I see." Myaisha studied her. Mrs. Lula was acting desperate to simply leave. *But why?* They had a comfortable friendship, discussing books and movies while baking or cooking. Something had upset Mrs. Lula, and Myaisha wanted to know what.

"A couple nights after you left, I thought I saw a light on in your house."

The septuagenarian listened raptly.

"I checked the windows and doors but found no evidence anyone tampered with your stuff. Inside, the house looked fine."

"Anything moved?"

"I didn't notice any disturbance, but I haven't been in your house often enough to know."

The senior appeared to be weighing the comments. Then she blurted out, "Anything else?"

"Quiet since then."

"Yes. Well…" She turned to leave. At the door, she hesitated. "Thank you." She gave Myaisha a tight hug and kiss on the cheek. "You're a great neighbor."

A sob caught in Myaisha's throat at the sudden embrace. "Welcome," she muttered.

"How long has the memorial been going on?" Mrs. Lula said, looking toward Roger's house.

"People have been stopping by all day." She took a few steps outside. "Roger worshiped Abigail."

"Humph." Mrs. Lula tightened the scarf around her neck. "I suppose taking her life made more sense than suffering in prison. Abigail wouldn't have survived confinement, even for a short time."

"She believed her motives were true."

Under Mrs. Lula's hard glare, Myaisha flinched.

"You don't believe she killed Jared to protect Patsy and those kids, do yah?"

"I…uh." Myaisha stuttered. "Roger believed his wife."

"More fool him." Mrs. Lula glanced around Myaisha at the front door. "I heard Abigail left a note on your door Monday night."

"And who told you that?"

"Allen." Mrs. Lula buttoned up her coat. "The old bag might cough up a hair ball, but she doesn't miss much."

I wonder if she observed Abigail sneaking around with Jared.

"The police didn't find the gardener." Mrs. Lula winked. "That detective of yours isn't as smart as I thought. Practically told him who did it before I left."

Myaisha's eyes widened. "You knew?"

"Wasn't hard to figure out."

"Why didn't you say anything?"

"Not my business. Besides, I couldn't stand Jared. His wife is better off without him."

"Mrs. Lula, you astound me."

"You're plenty clever too. Glad to know someone else can keep a secret." The old lady headed home.

Curious about what she meant, Myaisha ran inside to get a jacket and catch up with her. But despite her age, the old lady had made it inside her house before Myaisha reached the end of the driveway.

Mrs. Lula walked fast and had an even quicker perception. However, she was also worried. About what, would bother Myaisha until she had the answer. It would have to come from Mrs. Lula though. That woman could keep secrets.

CHAPTER 44

Securing the package under her arm, Myaisha knocked on the front door. Scampering and whining preceded the door opening. Zoey leaped on her legs.

"Down girl," AJ said, petting the Lab.

Boomer zipped inside. He and Zoey scampered around the living room.

"Well, you made their Friday night." He shut the door behind her.

Myaisha handed him the package.

His eyebrow arched questioningly.

"Open it."

He set the box down and helped Myaisha off with her coat.

Ever the gentleman. *Is this what Abigail resented in her husband?* Roger treated her too kindly.

Certain women didn't like men opening their car doors or helping them into chairs. *How did she feel? Was chivalry dead, antiquated, or misogynistic?*

"Can I get you something to drink?"

She followed him into the living room. A U-shaped black leather couch faced a huge wall-mounted television screen.

"Wine?" he asked, holding up a bottle.

"White."

He joined her in the living room after retrieving the package. "When you cancelled the weekly card game, I didn't expect to see you."

Without replying, Myaisha walked over to the wall of glass windows looking over the backyard. Outside, Boomer and Zoey chased each other, mindless of the cooling evening. Myaisha's back stiffened as AJ came up behind her.

She said, "About Christmas…"

A moment passed before he said, "I'm sorry", at the same time she said, "I apologize."

They smiled into each other's eyes.

He tipped his glass forward, and they clinked their drinks.

"To forgiveness."

Turning aside, Myaisha set her glass down on a side table. AJ retrieved a remote control and Peabo Bryson's *I'm So Into You* filled the room.

"Tell me what I did—what I can do to make things right."

She shook her head. "It's not you."

His face caved. "Did you drive across town to tell me you're the problem, and we should break up?"

Tears formed along her lashes. "I love you."

AJ's head rested on hers. Tilting her face upward, he rubbed his face alongside her cheeks. "Love you too."

Myaisha broke away. "I…" She swallowed hard and shook off her fears.

Her words came fast. "I relied on Sammy so much, and when he died my life collapsed." She rested on the edge of a chair, shuddering. "At night, I couldn't sleep. I kept feeling around the bed for his body. I didn't eat."

She rubbed her arms. "We ate breakfast together each morning. No more. Traveling with my trusted companion. No more." Myaisha gazed up at AJ through eyes blurred by tears. "We had been together for over twenty years. I…I had to learn how to live again, without him."

Rubbing her back, AJ led her to the couch. "My marriage didn't last half as long as yours, but I know what it's like to have to readjust after the person you loved is no longer around. It's not the same, but I understand loss."

Myaisha rested her head on his shoulder. "I'm afraid of depending on you too much."

AJ rested beside her and pulled her close. "When my wife left, I trashed the house and crashed my car."

She regarded his profile.

"It hurt—pissed me off. I took out my anger on objects, became self-destructive."

Myaisha entwined her fingers with his.

"It took time, but I cleaned up my act and reentered life. Living well became a path toward closing that chapter of my life."

She nodded, gazing at the rug.

He kissed her fingers. "If we lose each other, there are people who care for us and will support us through anything."

They gazed into each other's eyes and slowly their faces came closer. Barking interrupted their kiss.

AJ sighed. "Guess they finally got cold."

While he locked up, Myaisha changed the song to Stevie Wonder's *As*. She fed the dogs, washed up, and prepared snacks for her and AJ.

Opening the gift box, AJ exclaimed, "History videos!"

"A peace offering." She kissed his cheek. "I know how much you enjoy documentaries."

"Um, where to begin." He scanned the box contents. "Let's see. *Eyes on the Prize*. The original Alex Haley's *Roots*. Nice."

Myaisha rested on the sectional and clicked off the music. She turned on the television and asked, "What do you want to watch first?"

"Would you like more wine?" he asked, bringing the bottle over to the sofa.

Playfully smiling up into his eyes, she crossed her legs. "Sure. I'm not going anywhere."

Taking the remote from her hand, AJ switched off the television set and restarted the music player with Marvin Gaye. "Well, then. Let's get it on."

Thank you for reading *Murder Between Neighbors*. As a self-published author, I depend upon reviews to increase my visibility and credibility. Please post an honest review. Visit my website for book reviews and resources for writers.

If you missed the other books in the series, read *Murder Is Revealing* and *Murder In Gemini*. Sign up for my Write Club Mysteries newsletter and receive bonus content, information on new releases, and resources from the writing community.

For those who enjoy thrillers read *Hollow Voices*, a psychological thriller.

Mwindaji is for paranormal and horror readers. Check out *Dark Blood Awakens*, the first book in the series.